BLUFORD

BLACK ✦ STARS
OF
CIVIL WAR TIMES

BLACK ✦ STARS
OF
CIVIL WAR TIMES

✦

written by

JIM HASKINS
CLINTON COX
OTHA RICHARD SULLIVAN, ED. D.
ELEANORA TATE
BRENDA WILKINSON

JIM HASKINS, GENERAL EDITOR

John Wiley & Sons, Inc.

For general information about our other products and services, please contact our Customer Care Department within the United States at (800) 762-2974, outside the United States at (317) 572-3993 or fax (317) 572-4002.

Wiley also publishes its books in a variety of electronic formats. Some content that appears in print may not be available in electronic books. For more information about Wiley products, visit our web site at www.wiley.com.

ISBN 0-471-22069-8

Printed in the United States of America

10 9 8 7 6 5 4 3 2 1

Contents

INTRODUCTION

✦

The Civil War began in 1861, but the seeds of that long and drawn out conflict between the states were planted some two hundred years earlier. Slavery had long been a source of controversy among the American colonies. Although slaves were employed in both Northern and Southern colonies, the agriculture-based Southern colonies became highly dependent on their labor. Slaves in the North tended to be few by comparison and were more likely to be educated and learn skilled trades.

By the time the American colonies won their independence from England, many Northerners believed that a free land should not allow slavery. Most Southerners, however, were determined to maintain it. To reach a consensus on uniting the thirteen states under one federal government, the writers of the U.S. Constitution chose to ignore the paradox of slavery in a free nation. The words *slave* and *slavery* do not appear anywhere in the U.S. Constitution or in the Bill of Rights (the first ten amendments to that document). Instead, there are references to "persons owing service or labor." The new nation was established without a unified stand on slavery. Over the next decades, as new states joined the Union, debates raged over whether they should be admitted as slave states or free states. The issue of slavery in the United States was finally settled by a war that tore the nation apart.

African Americans, slave and free, played important roles in that war, as well as in events that led up to it. Throughout the nation, the number of free blacks rose steadily as slaves purchased their freedom or were granted it, pursued education, and acquired property. Free blacks in the North campaigned for the abolition of slavery and assisted runaway slaves from the South who took their future in their own hands and escaped to the free states and Canada.

Eventually, all attempts to compromise over the issue of slavery and keep the Union together failed. Seven Southern states left the Union to form the Confederate States of America, and a civil war resulted. Blacks were determined to be part of the fight. Despite the fact that many Northern whites did not want blacks to serve in the Union army, calling the conflict a "white man's war," African Americans persisted and, in the end, tipped the balance in favor of the Union side.

Union troops occupied the vanquished Confederate states in the aftermath of the Civil War. Blacks also played important roles during that period, which was called Reconstruction. Sixteen African Americans were elected to Congress from the South. Many more served in Southern legislatures and helped write new state constitutions guaranteeing free public education for all. After ten years, however, the occupying Union troops withdrew, returning the South to former slave owners and pro-slavery people. Most freedmen and women wound up working for their former owners or for other whites under a sharecropping system that was little better than slavery.

The people who are profiled in this book distinguished themselves in one way or another throughout the Civil War era. Some succeeded against great odds in business or the professions. Some fought for the abolition of slavery, while others helped escaped slaves find their way to freedom. Some served in the Union military during the war, and others tried to build a new, free South. Some of their names are still well known today, while others have been largely forgotten. All were people who actively sought to control their own lives, even those whose circumstances made that nearly impossible. Together, their stories make up an important, and often little known, chapter in American history.

SOJOURNER
TRUTH

(1797–1883)

Before the Civil War, most slaves faced endless days of labor and harsh treatment. Slaves who dared show defiance were subjected to severe beatings and other savage acts of punishment. Many blacks risked all by running away. Among those who ran was the bold and brave woman who came to be known as Sojourner Truth.

Sojourner Truth was born in Ulster County, New York, in 1797. Her name was Isabella, and she was owned by a Dutchman named Ardinburgh. During her youth, she was separated from her parents and passed among a succession of cruel masters, two of whom were named Baumfree and Hurley. Tall of stature and large of frame, she was exploited for her size and made to work excessively hard.

Sojourner watched her mother's grief as her siblings were sold away to other masters. She grew up to experience the same horror, giving birth to children only to have them torn from her arms. It is not known how many children she had, but when she escaped in 1826, she took only an infant son with her.

Fleeing with her child in the middle of night, Sojourner crept through dangerous forests and swamps, terrified of being tracked by bloodhounds and bounty hunters. She knew what could happen if she was caught alive. Punishment for escapees ranged from beatings, after which a solution of salt and vinegar was poured on open wounds, to the cutting off of body parts, such as toes and fingers. Sojourner clutched her infant tightly. A baby could not understand the need to be silent in the face of miseries that may have included unbearable heat or cold, bites of various insects, and insufficient food and water.

As Sojourner and other slaves stole their way through the nights, sympathizers—both black and white—risked their own safety, giving shelter, food, and water along the way. With such help, Sojourner made her way safely to New York, where slavery was outlawed the following year, 1827.

In 1843, while working as a maid in New York City, Sojourner became convinced that she had been called to go out into the world and "travel about the land spreading truth to the people." Changing her name to Sojourner Truth, she became a preacher. Sojourner testified. Describing the suffering she had lived through, she soon became a major spokesperson for the abolitionist movement. Along with Frederick Douglass and William Lloyd Garrison, she became a significant leader in the struggle for emancipation.

Some people mocked her and spread rumors that she was a man disguised in women's garments. To dispel those rumors, she once publicly exposed her breast, then told the stunned audience, "It is not my shame, but yours that I should do this."

Nothing could stop Sojourner Truth. One day as she attended a women's rights meeting in Akron, Ohio, clergymen argued that women should not have the right to vote. One dared to say that the fact that Christ was a man proved that God considered women inferior to men. Sojourner rose to speak. Some of the suffragettes worried that a former slave was not a proper spokesperson for them and would only bring ridicule to their cause. They gestured for her to return to her seat. But the president of the group, Frances Dana Gage, ignored them and welcomed Sojourner to the podium.

"Ain't I a Woman?," the courageous speech Sojourner gave that day, June 21, 1851, became etched in American history.

An acclaimed white author of the era, Harriet Beecher Stowe, wrote a special tribute to Sojourner in the *Atlantic Monthly*. In the 1863 article, Stowe said, "I do not recollect ever to have been conversant with any one who had more of that silent and subtle power which we call person presence than this woman."

During the Civil War, Sojourner Truth helped recruit soldiers and aided in relief efforts for freed men and women escaping from the South. As an adviser to President Abraham Lincoln, she used her influence to bring about the desegregation of streetcars in Washington, D.C.

"AIN'T I A WOMAN?"

"That man over there says that women need to be helped into carriages and lifted over ditches, and to have the best help everywhere. Nobody ever helps me into carriages, or over mud-puddles, or gives me any best place. Well, I'm a woman, ain't I?

"Look at my arms. I have ploughed, and planted, and gathered into barns, and no man could head me! And ain't I a woman?

"I could work as much and eat as much as a man, when I could get it—and bear the lash as well. And ain't I a woman?

"I have borne . . . children, and seen most all sold off to slavery, and when I cried out with a mother's grief, none but Jesus heard me! And ain't I a woman?"

—Sojourner Truth

One of Sojourner Truth's many roles was as an adviser to President Lincoln. They are shown here examining the Bible presented to them by people of Baltimore. Lincoln appointed her counselor to the Freedmen of Washington, a position she held until her retirement in 1875.

Sojourner Truth never learned to read or write, but she often said, "I cannot read a book, but I can read the people." In 1850, with the help of friends and family, she worked with Olive Gilbert to write and publish *Narrative of Sojourner Truth*; and she updated it with the assistance of Frances Titus. The expanded version, *Book of Life*, includes personal letters, newspaper stories of events in which she participated, and expressions of appreciation for her work sent to her from around the world. The narrative was reprinted in 1878, 1881, and 1884 with the title *Narrative of Sojourner Truth; A Bondswoman of Olden Time, With a History of Her Labors and Correspondence Drawn from Her "Book of Life."*

Sojourner Truth, one of America's greatest reformers, died at her home in Battle Creek, Michigan, in 1883.

TELL THAT STORY—THE ORAL TRADITION

Accounts of frightful journeys and all the horrors of slavery are known today largely because slaves passed those stories on through the "oral tradition" of storytelling. This became the means through which people without formal education helped preserve their histories and cultures until the day that someone else could write them down. Fortunately, Africans brought their oral traditions with them from their native cultures.

SARAH MAPPS
DOUGLASS

(1806–1882)

In the early nineteenth century the vast majority of African Americans were denied even a rudimentary education. The teaching of slaves was illegal throughout the South. Opportunities in the North were few, but some African American families managed to educate themselves and others. Sarah Mapps Douglass, who was born in Philadelphia on September 9, 1806, came from such a family.

Her mother's father, Cyrus Bustill, opened a school in his home in Philadelphia shortly after the Revolutionary War. He also helped found the Free African Society, which was the first African American benevolent society in the new nation. Bustill served as an example to his daughter Grace. When Grace grew up, she joined with wealthy black shipbuilder James Forten to start a school for black children in Philadelphia.

Grace Bustill married Robert Douglass, who was one of the founders of the First African Presbyterian Church. The Douglass family made sure that their children received an exceptionally good education. Sarah Douglass had tutors for several years, and was then

enrolled in her mother's school. Sarah Douglass, following in her mother's footsteps, opened her own school sometime in the 1820s. It was one of ten black schools in Philadelphia at the time.

Like her forebears, Douglass was active on many other fronts in the fight for racial equality. She was a member of the Philadelphia Female Anti-Slavery Society's board of directors and attended several abolitionist conventions. Her work in the society, which her mother and sixteen other women helped found in 1833 for the purpose of helping escaped slaves, led to friendships with some of the nation's leading white abolitionists, including members of the religious group known as the Quakers.

The Quakers, who had founded the colony of Pennsylvania, practiced racial discrimination, but most were against slavery and supported black education. In 1853, Sarah Douglass accepted a position as

IT TOOK COURAGE TO BE A TEACHER

In the South, increasingly harsh laws made it illegal to teach free or enslaved black people. These laws were driven by fear, and became even harsher after the uprisings led by Denmark Vesey in 1822 and Nat Turner in 1831. Both men were slaves who had learned to read and write. White Southerners were convinced that education had turned those men into dangerous revolutionaries willing to risk their lives to end slavery.

Despite the harsh laws, many African Americans in the South attended clandestine schools or managed to find a brave individual who secretly taught them to read and write.

Even in the North, there was often deep opposition to anyone who believed in educating black people. When future abolitionist and clergyman Henry Highland Garnet and two other black students arrived at the Noyes Academy in Canaan, New Hampshire, in 1834, an infuriated mob tore down the school rather than allow black students to attend.

head of the girls' primary department in the Quaker-supported Institute for Colored Youth in Philadelphia. This school is now known as Cheyney State University of Pennsylvania.

In 1855, Sarah married the Reverend William Douglass, rector of St. Thomas Protestant Episcopal Church. He passed away in 1861, at the start of the Civil War. Sarah Douglass remained active in the cause of freedom. She served as vice-chairman of the Women's Pennsylvania Branch of the American Freedmen's Aid Commission established at the end of the Civil War.

Sarah Mapps Douglass died in Philadelphia on September 8, 1882. She had spent more than fifty years teaching black youth. Her life was a powerful testament to what a determined person could accomplish even in the segregated America of the mid-1800s.

Many of the young people she taught, and the generations of students that many of them went on to teach, shared her belief that education could be a powerful force in fighting segregation and racism.

MAJOR MARTIN ROBISON
DELANY

(1812–1885)

The search for education led the parents of Martin Robison Delany from Virginia to Pennsylvania. Delany attended schools in Pittsburgh. He studied nights at a black church while also working during the day, and he received medical training from two local physicians. When he moved for a time to the Southwest in the late 1830s, he worked as a physician's assistant and dentist. Years later, Delany decided to pursue formal medical studies. He was one of the first blacks admitted to Harvard Medical School. He did not graduate, however, because his fellow students petitioned successfully for his dismissal. After leaving Harvard, Delany returned to Pittsburgh, where he became a leading physician and an activist in the anti-slavery cause. He started an abolitionist newspaper and later edited the newspaper published by the famous abolitionist Frederick Douglass.

Delany despaired that even whites who favored abolition would never accept blacks as equals. He began to give serious thought to the idea of blacks leaving the United States and seeking a life of peace and equality elsewhere. At first, he advocated emigration to Haiti or

THE ABOLITIONIST

In Pittsburgh, Martin Delany started a weekly newspaper, *The Mystery*. He published it from 1843 to 1846. In its pages, he championed equal rights for both blacks and women. He also worked to move fugitive slaves north and to restore the vote to blacks in Pennsylvania.

Through his work, Martin Delany became friendly with the noted abolitionist Frederick Douglass. Even the great Douglass noticed Delany's fierce black pride. Douglass said, "I thank God for making me a man simply, but Delany always thanks Him for making him a black man."[1]

In 1847, Douglass invited Delany to be an editor of Douglass's weekly newspaper, *North Star*, published in Rochester, New York. Delany was listed on the masthead as an editor until 1849.

Central America, later to Africa. In 1854, he organized a National Emigration Convention of 100 men and women—the first women to be accepted as delegates to a black convention.

In 1856, in protest against oppressive conditions for blacks in the United States, Delany moved to Canada, where he continued his medical practice. In 1858, he presided over an emigration convention in Chatham, Canada. The convention appointed Delany as chief commissioner of a Niger River exploration party. Accompanied by Robert Campbell, a young schoolteacher from Philadelphia, Delany spent nine months in Africa, exploring the Niger River delta region. He made an agreement with the rulers of Ahbeokuta, in present-day Nigeria, for an African American settlement there. For his leadership of this expedition, and for his writings on black equality, Delany became known as the Father of Black Nationalism.

In 1861, Delany returned to the United States and joined other black leaders in urging President Lincoln to enlist blacks to fight in the Civil War.

At the start of the Civil War, African Americans numbered 4 million enslaved and 480,000 free. After emancipation, thousands of black men joined the Union forces, sometimes followed by their families.

Two years later, in 1863, the War Department mustered the all-black Fifty-fourth Massachusetts Volunteer Regiment. Delany, among those most actively recruited, served as its surgeon.

In February 1865, Delany became the first black man to receive a regular army commission. Major Delany traveled to Hilton Head Island, South Carolina, to recruit and organize former slaves for the North. However, his efforts were cut short. The war ended in April with the surrender of Confederate General Robert E. Lee at Appomattox Court House, Virginia.

The federal government quickly sent occupying troops into the former Confederate states and established a period of Reconstruction, during which the Confederate states would write new constitutions.

These would guarantee equal rights to the former slaves when the Southern states were readmitted to the Union. The government also established a Freedman's Bureau to help the former slaves. Delany served on the bureau in South Carolina both before and after his honorable discharge from the army.

In 1874, Delany ran unsuccessfully as an Independent Republican for the office of lieutenant governor of South Carolina. He later became a customs inspector and trial justice in Charleston.

Delany continued his medical and scientific studies, publishing *Principia of Ethnology: The Origin of Race and Color* in 1879. He also published a novel, *Blake*. Major Delany died in Xenia, Ohio, on January 24, 1885.

LIEUTENANT PETER
VOGELSANG

(1815–1887)

Like Martin Delany, Peter Vogelsang became a commissioned officer in the all-black Fifty-fourth Massachusetts Volunteer Regiment. Born on August 21, 1815, in New York City, Vogelsang was working as a clerk when the Civil War broke out in April 1861.

At age forty-eight, Peter Vogelsang was by far the oldest recruit in the Fifty-fourth. Steady and serious, he soon became a father figure, particularly in Company H, one of the ten units into which the men were organized.

Vogelsang would have made a good commissioned officer from the start of his service. But the army was firmly against black recruits becoming officers. Governor Andrew of Massachusetts wrote to Secretary of War Stanton, asking for colored officers such as surgeons and a chaplain to be placed in colored regiments. But both Stanton and President Lincoln feared that appointing black officers would outrage whites. The average white Northerner was against slavery in principle, but had no interest in blacks having equal rights of citizenship.

"Who Would Be Free, Themselves Must Strike the Blow!"

$200 $200

COLORED MEN
Of Burlington Co.,

Your Country calls you to the Field of Martial Glory. Providence has offered you an opportunity to vindicate the Patriotism and Manhood of your Race. Some of your brothers accepting this offer on many a well-fought field, have written their names on history's immortal page amongst the bravest of the brave.

NOW IS YOUR TIME!

Remember, that every blow you strike at the call of your Government against this accursed Slaveholders' Rebellion, you Break the Shackles from the Limbs of your Kindred and their Wives and Children.

The Board of Freeholders of Burlington Co.

Now offers to every Able-Bodied COLORED MAN who volunteers in the Service of his Country a BOUNTY of

$200 CASH! $200
WHEN SWORN INTO THE SERVICE, and
$10 PER MONTH
WHILE IN SUCH SERVICE.   COME ONE! COME ALL!

RECRUITING THE FIFTY-FOURTH

No one could keep determined African Americans out of the war. Leading abolitionists like Martin Delany and Frederick Douglass continually pressed the cause. Escaped slaves made their way to Union lines and freedom. Union generals on the battlefields of the South found themselves suddenly responsible for the fugitives.

The Emancipation Proclamation turned the tide. It freed all slaves in the enemy states as of January 1, 1863. It declared that freed slaves "of suitable condition" would be "received into the armed service of the United States, to garrison forts, positions, stations, and other places, and to man vessels of all sorts."

Lincoln also agreed to enlist free blacks. Secretary of War Edwin M. Stanton authorized Governor John A. Andrew of Massachusetts to recruit and organize black soldiers into a regiment.

Abolitionists rushed to recruit for the new regiment. Frederick Douglass recruited his own sons—Charles, nineteen, and Lewis, twenty-two. The one thousand men who eventually made up the regiment came from twenty-two states, the District of Columbia, and the West Indies. The majority were in their twenties.

When the Fifty-fourth was mustered into service in March 1863, all twenty-nine officers were white. Colonel Robert Gould Shaw reported to General David Hunter in Hilton Head, South Carolina.

Barely had the Fifty-fourth made camp when Colonel James Montgomery ordered company H and seven others to travel farther south to Darien, Georgia. They watched as Union gunboats fired on the town. Then Montgomery ordered them to plunder and torch the houses. It was more like piracy than warfare. Shaw protested, but Montgomery was determined to destroy Darien. The men of the Fifty-fourth reluctantly followed orders.

Shaw promoted Peter Vogelsang almost as soon as the Fifty-

Attacking Fort Wagner, the Fifty-fourth Massachusetts valiantly faces Confederate artillery.

fourth Massachusetts reached the South, first to sergeant and then, on April 17, to quartermaster sergeant, both noncommissioned ranks. Ordinarily, that would have meant a raise in pay. But the Fifty-fourth Massachusetts did not operate under ordinary circumstances.

In early July, the Fifty-fourth Massachusetts joined other Union regiments in a campaign against Charleston, South Carolina. The regiment sailed north on the steamer *Chasseur.* On July 11, Vogelsang and his comrades debarked on James Island, off the coast of South Carolina, where several Confederate regiments waited. It was there that the Fifty-fourth Massachusetts came under fire for the first time.

Vogelsang not only stood fast but advanced, taking with him his whole company. Although he was wounded, he managed to accompany the Fifty-fourth to the next battle.

On July 16, 1863, the men of the Fifty-fourth were ordered to begin a forced march that lasted a day and a half. Their destination was Charleston, South Carolina, and their mission was to capture Fort Wagner, a Confederate stronghold guarding the entrance to Charleston Harbor. They had rested from their long march only about thirty minutes when Brigadier General George C. Strong, who had replaced Colonel Montgomery, gave the order for the charge. The column advanced. Immediately, the fort's big guns and muskets fired on them. Colonel Robert Gould Shaw was killed, but his men fought on.

Although the Fifty-fourth failed to capture the fort, the regiment proved its bravery. Northern newspapers made much of the battle and of the courage of the black troops. Union General Ulysses S. Grant, commander of all army forces, wrote to President Lincoln, "By arming the Negro we have added a powerful ally. They will make good soldiers and taking them from the enemy weakens him in the same proportion they strengthen us."[1]

Congress awarded fourteen members of the Fifty-fourth Massachusetts the Medal of Honor, established during the Civil War as the highest military award for bravery, for their courageous assault on Fort Wagner. That battle changed the attitude of many Northerners toward the black volunteers.

The Fifty-fourth Massachusetts continued to see action until the war ended in April 1865. Peter Vogelsang rose to second lieutenant and then first lieutenant—one of only three men in the Fifty-fourth to be commissioned as officers. On August 20, 1865, his term of service expired, Lieutenant Vogelsang returned to New York City and lived another twenty years. He died on April 4, 1887.

ELIZABETH
KECKLEY

(1818–1907)

Elizabeth Keckley had the unique distinction of sewing dresses for the wives of the men who served as president of the United States of America and president of the Confederate States of America. Born Elizabeth Hobbs to a slave family in Dinwiddie Courthouse, Virginia, she was only in her mid-teens when she was sold to a slaveowner in North Carolina and forced to leave her family. In her new place of enslavement in North Carolina, she was raped, probably by her owner, and later gave birth to a son. Then, when Elizabeth was eighteen, she and her son were repurchased by the daughter of her original owner, who took them to St. Louis, Missouri, to live.

In all probability, Elizabeth was sought out by a member of her original owner's family because of her exceptional skills as a seamstress. She started a dressmaking business in St. Louis that eventually became so prosperous that it supported her owners and their five children, as well as herself and her own son.

Elizabeth hated being a slave, and one reason she married James Keckley was that he claimed to be free. She later learned that he had

lied to her about his status. The couple separated, but Elizabeth kept his name for the rest of her life.

In 1855, when Elizabeth was thirty-seven years old, she borrowed money from her dressmaking clients to purchase her freedom for $1,200. She continued in business in St. Louis for another five years, until she had earned enough money to pay back the loans. She later purchased her son's freedom.

In 1860, Keckley moved first to Baltimore, Maryland, and then to Washington, D.C. In the nation's capital, she employed twenty girls and her clients included Mrs. Jefferson Davis, whose husband was at that time a senator from Mississippi. Introduced to Mary Todd Lincoln on the day after President Lincoln's inauguration, Keckley soon became the First Lady's dressmaker. Within months, seven southern states had seceded from the Union, and Keckley's former client, Mrs. Davis, became the First Lady of the Confederate States of America.

Elizabeth Keckley moved into the White House, serving as Mary Todd Lincoln's dressmaker, personal maid, and confidante.

In her free time, she worked with other black women to form an organization to aid former slaves seeking refuge in the capital. She secured donations from Mrs. Lincoln as well as from such prominent African American abolitionists as Frederick Douglass and Wendell Phillips. The Contraband Relief Association, as her organization was known, changed its name to the Freedmen and Soldier's Relief Association of Washington when blacks were allowed to join the Union army.

Keckley's son served in the Union army, but he did not have to wait until blacks were accepted. He was light-complected enough to serve in a white regiment. Sadly, he was killed in action.

After President Lincoln was assassinated in 1865, Mary Todd Lincoln and her children moved out of the White House. Keckley moved, too, but continued to make dresses for Mary Todd Lincoln and remained her close personal friend until 1868.

Mathew Brady took this formal photograph of Mary Todd Lincoln in 1861, one year after President Lincoln's inauguration. Elizabeth Keckley probably made this gown and styled Mrs. Lincoln's hair for the occasion. (National Archives)

Keckley spent her last years supported by a pension paid to her because her son had died fighting for the Union cause. The rest home in which she died on May 26, 1907, was one she had helped found for others.

FREDERICK
DOUGLASS

(1818–1895)

The life and career of Frederick Douglass spanned the entire Civil War era, and he was involved in all the activities that affected African Americans during that time. Born Frederick Bailey, a slave, on the eastern shore of Maryland, he escaped at the age of twenty-one and made his way to New Bedford, Massachusetts, where he worked as a stevedore on the docks of that port town. An imposing figure and a self-educated, eloquent speaker, he soon found himself in great demand at abolitionist meetings.

Settling in Rochester, New York, with his wife, Anna, Douglass traveled throughout the Northeast appearing at anti-slavery conventions. He also backed the cause of women's suffrage and was often a featured speaker at meetings in support of women's right to vote. From his base in Rochester, he published a series of newspapers in which he gave his views on issues affecting African Americans. One was entitled *North Star*, a reference to the way escaping slaves used the stars to guide them north to freedom. The very first issue of that newspaper

in 1847 stated that its editor was involved in Underground Railroad activity. He opened his home to fugitives as they made their way to Canada and gave them food and money to continue their journey.

In the early months of the Civil War, President Lincoln saw the goal of the struggle as the preservation of the Union. In his opinion, the question of slavery was secondary. He and his military advisers were reluctant to employ African Americans in combat. Douglass emphatically disagreed. The war was about slavery, he argued, and African Americans should be part of it. In a speech in the winter of 1861–1862, Douglass charged, "We are striking the guilty rebels with our soft, white hand, when we should be striking with the iron hand of the black man."[1] In the fall of 1862, Lincoln finally began to allow the enlistment of black troops. Douglass personally traveled to Boston with other noted abolitionists to urge African Americans to enlist in the Union army. His own sons, Charles, nineteen, and Lewis, twenty-two, joined up.

After the Union defeat of the Confederacy, Douglass moved to Washington, D.C., where he served in several appointive offices, including U.S. marshal for the District of Columbia; recorder of deeds for Washington, D.C.; and minister-general to the Republic of Haiti. While enjoying success and respect himself, he did not forget the former slaves in the South, for whom the initial promise of the Union victory proved empty. During the Reconstruction period that followed, the U.S. government attempted to prepare the former slaves for lives of freedom. But the freedmen, uneducated and unpropertied, were ill-equipped to live as free citizens, and government efforts to help them were too disorganized and short-lived. After ten years, the occupying federal troops pulled out of the former Confederate states, in effect leaving the hapless freedmen to the mercy of their former owners.

At his death in 1895, Frederick Douglass could not help but despair that his fellow African Americans would never enjoy true freedom and equality in the United States. At least he was spared the knowledge of the Supreme Court's 1896 decision in the case of *Plessy v. Ferguson* that separate accommodations for blacks (segregation) was constitutional.

TO THE WHIRLWIND

After Reconstruction ended, a weary Frederick Douglass summed it up in this way: "When you turned us loose, you gave us no acres. You turned us loose to the sky, to the storm, to the whirlwind, and, worst of all, you turned us loose to the wrath of our infuriated masters."[2]

HARRIET
TUBMAN
(1820–1913)

Harriet Tubman, one of the most famous conductors on the Underground Railroad often worked closely with Frederick Douglass. Tubman was born on the plantation of Edward Brodas in Dorchester County, Maryland. Her parents, Harriet Greene and Benjamin Ross, were enslaved. When she was born, she was named Araminta; but later she was called Harriet, after her mother. When Harriet was six, her owner hired her out to work for local people, who treated her cruelly. On the Brodas plantation, she received an injury that would cause her to suddenly lose consciousness at random times for the rest of her life. She had attempted to block the way of an overseer chasing after a slave who was trying to escape. A brick intended for the runaway hit her instead.

In 1848, Harriet married John Tubman, a freedman. When she confided in him that she wanted to escape, he threatened to report her. But when Harriet learned that she had been sold to a Georgia slave trader, she fled and made her way to Philadelphia. After two years in Philadelphia, Harriet learned that her sister and her sister's children

were about to be sold. She returned to Maryland to assist her sister's husband in rescuing his family from a slave pen in Cambridge, Maryland. Not long after that daring rescue, she returned to the Brodas plantation. She wanted to persuade her husband to join her in the North. Instead, she found that he had remarried. Undaunted, Harriet brought out eleven slaves, including one of her brothers and his wife.

By 1851, she had become a legend as a conductor on the Underground Railroad. She established a pattern that she maintained for six years, until 1857. Each year she made two trips to the South, one in the spring and one in the fall. She spent the winters in St. Catherine's, Ontario, where many fugitive slaves had settled, and the summers working in hotels in places such as Cape May, New Jersey, to earn money for her trips. In the spring of 1857, she managed to rescue her aged parents.

THE UNION SCOUT

In 1863, Tubman accompanied guerrilla fighter Colonel James Montgomery and about 800 African American soldiers of the Second South Carolina Volunteers on a gunboat raid along the Combahee River in South Carolina. She and her scouts surveyed the area and identified places where Confederate soldiers had placed explosives along the river. With this crucial information, the Union gunboats zigzagged up the river, avoiding the explosives and picking off small bands of Confederate soldiers. Meanwhile, Union troops made their way along both riverbanks, setting fire to plantation fields, dwellings, and stores of cotton.

Confederate troops retreated, and plantation families fled with them, taking as many slaves as they could. Some of the slaves saw their chance for freedom. They ran to the river from all directions, waving and shouting to the Union gunboats. The seamen took them aboard and back to Union camps. That expedition rescued more than 750 African Americans.

By the fall of 1858, Tubman had helped more than 300 slaves reach the North and freedom. She had come to be called Moses for leading her people to the promised land. By 1860, the reward for her capture was $40,000—a huge sum in those days. In December 1860, she made

A NURSE REMEMBERS

Another African American woman who devoted herself to helping win the war was Susie King Taylor (1848–1912). Born a slave on a plantation near Savannah, Georgia, she joined the First South Carolina Volunteers. Starting out as a laundress, she accepted other tasks with enthusiasm. In her memoirs, *Reminiscences of My Life in Camp* (1902), she wrote:

"I learned to handle a musket very well and could shoot straight and often hit the target. I assisted in cleaning the guns and used to fire them off, to see if the cartridges were dry, before cleaning and reloading. . . . [After a battle] I hastened down to the landing when the wounded began to arrive, some with their legs off, arm gone, foot off, and wounds of all kinds imaginable.

"There are many people who do not know what colored women did during the war. Hundreds of them assisted Union soldiers by hiding them and helping them to escape. Many were punished for taking food to the prison stockades for the prisoners . . . although they knew what the penalty would be should they be caught."[1]

Susie King Taylor, the first known black army nurse in American history, served with the First South Carolina Volunteers during the Civil War.

her last trip as a conductor on the Underground Railroad. By early 1861, the North and South were at war, and it was no longer possible to continue her trips south.

During the Civil War, Tubman served the Union cause in several ways. In May 1862, months before the first Northern black regiments were authorized, Tubman went to South Carolina with a group of missionary-teachers to aid the hundreds of escaped slaves who had made their way to Union lines after the Union fleet had captured the South Carolina sea islands. She helped the women start a laundry business and also nursed both soldiers and freedmen at the army hospital on the islands.

Tubman also recruited a group of former slaves as Union scouts. They hunted for Confederate camps and reported on enemy troop movements and on the locations of cotton warehouses, ammunition depots, and slaves waiting to be liberated.

After about two years of serving the Union, Tubman received word that her parents, old and in poor health, needed her attention. She traveled to Auburn, New York, where she had bought a home for them, and cared for them until she herself became ill. But Harriet was strong. Soon enough, she was back on her feet, working as matron of the Colored Hospital at Fortress Monroe.

After the war, Tubman tried, but failed, to secure a government pension for her service to the Union forces. So she started selling eggs and vegetables door-to-door. A neighbor helped her write her story, *Scenes from the Life of Harriet Tubman*. The book brought in a small income. In March 1869, she married Nelson Davis, more than twenty years her junior. He suffered from tuberculosis contracted during the war. Selfless as always, she cared for him until he died in 1888, at age forty-four. As his widow, she finally collected a military pension of $20 per month. She died on March 10, 1913.

FRANCES E. W.
HARPER

(1825–1911)

Frances Ellen Watkins Harper did not serve in the Civil War, but she wrote a novel about it. *Iola Leroy* (1892) was the best-selling novel by an African American in the nineteenth century. It is the saga of educated, light-skinned, free blacks who are sold into slavery. Iola and her brother join the Union army as a nurse and a soldier, respectively, and then reunite, older and much wiser, after the long Civil War.

Born on September 24, 1825, in Baltimore, Maryland, Frances Ellen Watkins was the spirited only child of free parents. Orphaned by age three, she was raised by an aunt and uncle. Frances's uncle was a minister, writer, and educator who made sure that his niece read the Bible and practiced writing every day. At age thirteen, Frances was hired out to do domestic work, but she continued to study during her leisure time.

Frances loved words and in 1845 published a book of poetry entitled *Forest Leaves*. Unfortunately, no copy of the book remains today. She continued to write and eventually produced four novels and numerous volumes of poetry, short stories, and essays during her long life.

Frances's first career was as a teacher. Hired as the first female teacher at Union Seminary, a school organized by the African Methodist Episcopal Church, she later taught in Little York, Pennsylvania.

Because of the fugitive slave laws, Frances Watkins and all free blacks traveling around the country risked being seized in any slave-holding state and declared a slave. Living with such restrictions frustrated her. And more than this, it troubled her to read news stories of those who suffered daily under slave codes and worse. Frances decided to resign from her teaching position in the 1850s and dedicate all her time to fighting slavery.

Writing became Frances's weapon. Her book, *Eliza Harris*, written in response to Harriet Beecher Stowe's 1853 publication, *Uncle Tom's Cabin*, brought praise from abolitionists Frederick Douglass and William Lloyd Garrison. Both men began reserving space for her protests in their publications. They also wrote introductions to some of her writings. Frances was hired as a speaker by the Maine Anti-Slavery Society, which led to other speaking invitations from abolitionist groups.

The author's publication of *Poems on Miscellaneous Subjects* in 1854 (which featured an introduction by William Lloyd Garrison) sold more than 10,000 copies in its first printing. Reprinted more than twenty times during her lifetime, it also became a favorite among young militant poets of the 1960s because of its fiery tone. Many young blacks were inspired to write poetry against segregation after discovering Frances Watkins's protest poems and essays.

As emancipation seemed further out of reach than ever, Frances Watkins grew more militant. When abolitionist John Brown failed in his attempt to start a slave rebellion at Harpers Ferry, Virginia (now West Virginia), in 1859, Frances led a campaign of support for him. There was no chance of securing the freedom of John Brown, his sons, or the black men who took part in the failed raid. But Frances felt she could at least write to the families of the men who awaited the gallows. She also helped raise financial support for the families. As Watkins wrote in a newspaper editorial, "It is not enough to express our sympathy by words. We should be ready to crystallize it into action."

In 1860, the author married Fenton Harper, a widower with three children. They lived on his farm in Columbus, Ohio, where Frances gave birth to a daughter. Fenton Harper died four years after their marriage. With debts absorbing most of her husband's assets, Frances Harper returned to the lecture circuit. She also became one of the many teachers who traveled south after the Civil War to teach newly freed slaves.

In her collection *Sketches of Southern Life* (1872), Harper created a sixty-year-old ex-slave, Aunt Chloe, a witty character who tells the story of slavery and Reconstruction—and how she triumphs in the end. The conversational style that Harper used to tell those stories would be used by future writers such as the famous poet Langston Hughes.

A Protest Poem

The Slave Auction
by Frances Harper

The sale began—young girls were there,
Defenseless in their wretchedness,
Whose stifled sobs of deep despair
Revealed their anguish and distress.

And mothers stood with streaming eyes,
And saw their dearest children sold;
Unheeded rose their bitter cries,
While tyrants bartered them for gold.

Frances Harper was cofounder and officer of the National Association of Colored Women and also served with the National Council of Women, the Universal Peace Union, the Women's Christian Temperance Union, and other clubs and organizations. She died of heart disease on February 20, 1911, and was eulogized at the Unitarian Church in Eden Cemetery, Philadelphia.

Dr. Alexander T.
AUGUSTA

(1825–1890)

Alexander Augusta, a physician like Martin Delany, also played an active role in the struggle for black equality in the Civil War era. Born free in Norfolk, Virginia, he learned to read in secret because Virginia law forbade teaching any black person to read. His teacher was Daniel Payne, who later became a bishop of the African Methodist Episcopal Church.

As a young man, Augusta moved to Baltimore, where he made his living as a barber. He used his earnings to pay for tutoring in medicine. Hoping to become a doctor, Augusta moved to Philadelphia to enroll in the University of Pennsylvania's medical school. Although his application was rejected because of his race, a professor at the school allowed Augusta to study medicine in his office.

Like many other black doctors in the nineteenth century, Augusta finally got his medical education at a foreign school, the University of Toronto's Trinity Medical College in Canada. Enrolling in 1850, Augusta graduated in 1856 with a Bachelor of Medicine degree. He stayed in Toronto for approximately six years, conducting a private

practice and heading the Toronto City Hospital. After a while, he quit the hospital in order to direct an industrial school. He continued his private practice in Canada, while gaining skills as an administrator.

A few months after the Civil War broke out, Augusta tried to join the Union army's volunteer medical service. Like other black doctors, he was turned down, but he refused to be discouraged. Finally, he appealed directly to President Lincoln, after Lincoln gave permission for black men to serve.

"I was compelled to leave my native country, . . . on account of prejudice against colour, for the purpose of obtaining a knowledge of my profession," he wrote the president on January 7, 1863, "and having accomplished that object . . . I would like to be in a position where I can be of use to my race."[1]

A month after finally being commissioned, Augusta boarded a train in his native land dressed in his uniform with the oak-leaf straps of a major. He was immediately attacked by several men who were enraged at the sight of a black officer. They punched him and tore off one of the straps. Augusta got off the train and went to the nearest provost guard. He reboarded the train under armed escort.

Augusta was assigned to the Seventh United States Colored Troops. The Seventh would go on to fight in ten major battles, including Deep Bottom, James Island, Bermuda Hundreds, Chapin's Farm, Petersburg, and Richmond. But Doctor Augusta spent only a few months with the regiment. He was transferred after six white surgeons and assistant surgeons protested serving under his command.

Reassigned to Baltimore to examine black recruits, Augusta retained his rank as surgeon in the Seventh and suffered more protests from white officers who were blocked from advancement because he outranked them.

Augusta's transfer from the regiment helped him make medical history. He was appointed to run Camp Barker, the forerunner of Freedmen's Hospital in Washington, D.C., thereby becoming the first black person in the United States to direct a government hospital. The hospital was established as the capital reeled from an influx of more than 30,000 escaped slaves, almost two-thirds of whom needed medical treatment.

Camp Barker was opened on a temporary basis to help these freedmen, and in 1868 Freedmen's Hospital was established to permanently "care for the national needs of Negroes who, because of the lack of facilities, were inadequately cared for in their respective states."[2]

At least 1 million black patients were treated by both black and white doctors in the more than 100 hospitals and dispensaries set up by the Freedmen's Bureau during the Civil War, including Camp Barker. When the war ended, African American doctors and nurses were more desperately needed than ever—a need the hospitals and dispensaries of the Freedmen's Bureau had partially filled during the war.

Augusta spent several months after the war in charge of a hospital in Savannah, Georgia. In 1868, he was elected to the faculty of the newly organized medical department of Howard University to teach anatomy, becoming the first black faculty member in an American medical school. Augusta also served on the staff of Freedmen's Hospital until 1877.

Augusta left Freedmen's in 1877 to set up a private practice in Washington. He maintained the practice until his death on December 21, 1890.

Dr. Alexander T. Augusta was buried in Arlington National Cemetery, the final resting place of so many of the nation's heroes. It was a fitting honor for the man who had been so determined to serve his country and his cause.

JOHN P.
PARKER

(1827–1900)

✦

Born just two years after Alexander T. Augusta, John P. Parker had a radically different life. While Augusta was born free and managed to gain a medical education, Parker was born a slave and never attended school. Both men, however, worked for their people in their own ways during the Civil War era.

Parker was the son of a slave woman and her white owner in Norfolk, Virginia. He never knew his father, and he was sold away from his mother at the age of eight and taken to the Deep South. He had his first bit of good luck in Mobile, Alabama: instead of being sold to a plantation owner for back-breaking work in the cotton fields, he was purchased by a doctor to serve as a driver and as a servant and playmate to the doctor's two young sons.

Life was comparatively good for Parker as a slave in the doctor's household. Although Alabama law prohibited teaching slaves to read and write, the doctor's sons shared their lessons with Parker and smuggled books to him from the family library. When it came time for the boys to go off to college, Parker was delighted to learn that he

would accompany them to Yale University in New Haven, Connecticut. He was 16 years old and eager to get his own—unofficial—college education.

On the trip north, the doctor and his sons and Parker stopped off in Philadelphia, which happened to be a hotbed of abolitionist feeling at the time. Local abolitionists approached Parker with an offer of help to escape, but he was so naive that he reported the incident to his owner. The doctor decided not to send him to New Haven with the boys and took him back to Mobile.

Angry and resentful, Parker tried to run away, got into fights, and otherwise caused problems for his owner, who decided to sell him. Parker persuaded an elderly patient of the doctor's to buy him, promising in turn to purchase his freedom from her. He earned the money by working in a local iron foundry.

Once he had secured his own freedom, Parker headed north to the free state of Ohio, settling in the town of Ripley, just across the Ohio River from Kentucky, a slave state. He supported himself with jobs as an iron moulder. He got involved in Underground Railroad work when a fellow in the boarding house where he lived asked his help in freeing two young slave girls across the state border in Kentucky. After a harrowing but successful rescue mission, Parker decided it was his purpose in life to help other enslaved people to

A DARING RESCUE

One of Parker's most exciting and dangerous adventures was the rescue of a slave couple and their infant. The couple's owner suspected they might try to escape and took the infant into his and his wife's bedroom at night. Parker sneaked into the house and stole the baby away. By that time, authorities in Kentucky had offered a reward of $1,000 for him, dead or alive.

escape. From then on he led a double life, going about his usual business by day and serving as a conductor on the Underground Railroad at night. He later claimed that by 1850 he had assisted 315 runaways. Usually, he helped small groups, but once he actually took on the risky task of conducting a group of ten to free soil and managed to lead eight to safety.

Underground Railroad work was dangerous. Parker had to worry about being caught by slave owners, hunted by slave catchers, and reported by spies in the employ of slave owners and other people who supported slavery. He did not cease his activity, however, until the outbreak of the Civil War.

After the war began, Parker helped to raise a regiment of escaped slaves to assist the Union forces. He then concentrated on his own life and work. Married and the father of six children, he owned and operated a foundry and woodworking shop. There he invented a new type of tool to break up hard-packed soil and also a tobacco press. He was one of fifty-five African Americans to receive government patents before 1901.

In the 1880s, a reporter for the *Chattanooga* (Tennessee) *News* interviewed Parker about his Underground Railroad activity and wrote a manuscript entitled "The Autobiography of John P. Parker." The manuscript was still unpublished when Parker died in 1900.

In the middle 1980s, 100 years after Parker told his story to the newspaper reporter, historians began to try to document and preserve sites associated with the Underground Railroad. The manuscript of John P. Parker's story was rediscovered and published in 1996. Proceeds from the sale of the book were used to restore the house where Parker had lived with his family in Ripley, Ohio, and it was turned into the home of the John P. Parker Historical Society.

FRANCIS LOUIS
CARDOZO

(1837–1903)

The southern schools in which black teachers conducted classes were often old cotton barns, sheds, kitchens, and even tents. One of the most urgent tasks of black men and women throughout the newly liberated areas of the Confederacy was providing adequate school buildings and teachers for their children. During 1867, black men and women built twenty-three schoolhouses in South Carolina and contributed $12,200 to pay the teachers.

The Freedmen's Bureau, along with northern societies and church groups, also supplied schools and teachers for black children in many southern states. By 1870, there were more than 9,000 teachers and 247,000 pupils in both day and night schools supported by bureau funds.

One of the most successful of the new schools was Avery Institute in Charleston, South Carolina. The school was opened in 1865 with financial support from the American Missionary Association (AMA), which hired many of the teachers who came south.

The man who founded Avery and was its first principal was one of the leading black educators and political figures of his day: Francis

52

Louis Cardozo. Cardozo was born free in Charleston on February 1, 1837, to a Jewish journalist and economist, Jacob N. Cardozo, and a mother who was half black and half Native American. He attended school only from the ages of five to twelve. Then, like most children of his day, he left school to learn a trade. He worked as a carpenter's apprentice for five years and as a carpenter for four more.

Determined to receive an advanced education and become an ordained minister, Cardozo worked hard and saved his money to enroll in the University of Glasgow in Scotland. He supported himself by doing carpentry.

During a competitive examination with students from the University of Glasgow and three other colleges, Cardozo won a $1,000 scholarship. After four years at Glasgow, he continued his studies at Presbyterian seminaries in Edinburgh and London for three more years.

Cardozo returned to the United States during the Civil War, and in 1864 was named pastor of the Temple Street Congregational Church in New Haven, Connecticut. He married Catherine Rowena Howell of New Haven that same year, and the couple eventually had four sons and two daughters.

In 1865, at war's end, Cardozo moved back to Charleston to establish Avery Institute and begin his pioneering work in black education in the South. The Avery Institute was located in a building that had housed the state's teacher training school. Cardozo hired twenty teachers, ten black and ten white. On October 1, 1865, the first day of school, more than 1,000 students enrolled. The building was so crowded that more than 100 students had to be taught in the dome at the top of the building.

Cardozo had established the school to teach only the earliest grades. Most of the freedmen's schools were organized this way. Many of Avery's students, however, were from Charleston's free black population and already had some education. Cardozo soon initiated

THE BIRTH OF BLACK COLLEGES

Cardozo's introduction of advanced courses at Avery coincided with efforts to establish black colleges in other parts of the South. The North already had three black colleges: the Institute for Colored Youth in Philadelphia, which grew into Cheyney State University (1837); Lincoln University in Lincoln, Pennsylvania (1854); and Wilberforce University in Wilberforce, Ohio (1856).

When Avery opened, the AMA also helped organize Atlanta University in Atlanta, Georgia, then followed with the founding of other black colleges: Talladega College in Talladega, Alabama, in 1867; Hampton Institute (to train black farmers) in Hampton, Virginia, in 1868; and Tougaloo College in Tougaloo, Mississippi, in 1869.

Fisk University, which the AMA helped found in Nashville, Tennessee, in 1867, was originally housed in old army barracks. Spelling books and Bibles were bought with money raised from the sale of iron handcuffs and chains from the slave pens in Nashville. In the first year of its existence, 1,000 students enrolled.

more advanced courses for those children, including classics, Latin, and higher mathematics.

One man who visited the school less than two months after it opened said he found "the scholars studious and very orderly, and at all stages of advancement. In a room . . . three hundred children together were taking an object lesson; in another room a class of boys, whose parents, I was told, intended them for professional life, were transposing, analyzing, and parsing a passage from Milton's 'L'Allegro,' and recitations in reading and arithmetic were going on with more or less success before the other teachers."[1]

In 1868, Cardozo was elected as a delegate to the state constitutional convention, which was required under the Reconstruction Acts passed by the federal government. Cardozo served as chairman of the committee on education, and it was in this role that he helped plan a system of public schools for South Carolina, which his fellow delegates voted to approve.

That same year, and again in 1870, Cardozo was elected as South Carolina's secretary of state. He was the first black person in the United States elected to a state cabinet office. He was elected state treasurer in 1872 and 1874. The end of Reconstruction in 1877, and the return of white domination and the oppression that followed, ended his political career.

Returning to Washington, Cardozo helped educate many more black students while serving as principal of the Colored Preparatory High School from 1884 to 1891, and of the M Street High School from 1891 to 1896.

Francis Louis Cardozo died in Washington on July 22, 1903, after decades of working to improve the education of African American children. In 1928, a business high school was named in his honor in the nation's capital. His greatest legacy, however, was the public school system he helped establish in South Carolina and the countless children of all races who received an education because of his efforts.

GOVERNOR
PINCKNEY BENTON STEWART
PINCHBACK

(1837–1921)

While Francis Cardozo was the first black state office holder, P. B. S. Pinchback was the first black American to serve as a state lieutenant governor.

Pinchback was born free on May 10, 1837, in Macon, Georgia. He was the eighth child of Eliza Stewart and Major William Pinchback, a white Mississippi planter. Eliza Stewart had been enslaved when her seven other children were born, but by the time of Pinckney's birth, she had been freed. When Pinckney and his older brother, Napoleon, were nine and sixteen, respectively, their father sent them to Gilmore's School in Cincinnati. After eighteen months, they were called home because Major Pinchback was dying. On his death, his relatives seized his estate. Fearing that they might attempt to re-enslave her and her children, Eliza Stewart fled. She went to Cincinnati with her five youngest children—Napoleon, Mary, Pinckney, Adeline, and a baby girl.

Napoleon soon proved mentally unfit to work. So at the age of twelve Pinckney became the primary support of his family. He

P. B. S. PINCHBACK.
EX-GOVERNOR OF LOUISIANA.

signed on as a cabin boy on the canal boats running between Cincinnati and Miami, Toledo, Ohio, and Fort Wayne, at a salary of $8 a month. Hardworking and smart, he was eventually promoted to steward. In 1860, he married Nina Emily Hawthorne, whom he had met in Memphis.

After the Confederates fired on Fort Sumter in 1861, Pinchback started looking for a way to get into the fight on the Union side. He found it in New Orleans, a cosmopolitan city with a large population of free blacks. Union navy admiral David Farragut had captured New Orleans in 1862. Soon after, Major General Benjamin J. Butler put out a call for a regiment of black soldiers, the Corps d'Afrique, for the Louisiana National Guard. Pinchback jumped at the chance to join the military. He traveled to New Orleans, where he set about recruiting a company.

The enthusiastic twenty-four-year-old managed to raise an entire company in just over a week. The Second Louisiana Native Guards entered into service for the Union on October 12, 1862, under the command of Captain P. B. S. Pinchback.

In contrast to the Union army in the North, in Louisiana, at first, black troops could serve under black officers. All three of the regiments—the First, Second, and Third Louisiana Native Guards (unlike the other regiments, the last was composed of former slaves)—had black officers.

The black regiments distinguished themselves in battle, but that did not ensure the military future of their black officers. Pinchback and the other black officers learned that their commissions were merely temporary, pending qualification examinations. In the next few months, one by one they were disqualified and mustered out. Their places were taken by white officers. Of all the original black officers of the Corps d'Afrique, only Pinchback qualified.

Pinchback was determined to have the respect he deserved as a Union officer. He refused to ride on the New Orleans streetcars marked

UNDER ENEMY FIRE

The black units saw their first combat during May and June of 1863. The long battle of Port Hudson, Louisiana, included two Louisiana Native Guard regiments and six Corps d'Afrique regiments. Officers, white and black, had stories to tell of the brave black soldiers.

Captain Pinchback's men incurred severe injuries, but rejoined the fray rather than go to a field hospital. With exceptional determination, they kept advancing when certain to be assaulted by enemy fire. Major General Banks reported on the black troops: "The severe test to which they were subjected, and the determined manner in which they encountered the enemy, leaves upon my mind no doubt of their ultimate success."[1]

with a large star for "colored" passengers. Whenever he rode a streetcar, he rode alone—the car blocked off so that no white passenger could board. No direct action was taken against Pinchback. Instead, he was denied the opportunity to rise in the ranks of the Corps d'Afrique. Twice he was passed over for promotion.

By September 1863, Pinchback had had enough. He was much too proud to allow the situation to continue. He submitted his letter of resignation.

After the Union victory in the Civil War, the federal government was anxious for the former Confederate states to rejoin the Union. But after southerners began to pass a series of laws known as "Black Codes" to limit African American rights, Congress passed the Reconstruction Act of 1867. This law placed ten southern states under military law and established universal male suffrage, meaning that all men could vote. Republicans gained control of the Reconstruction state governments and encouraged blacks both to vote and seek political office.

Pinchback entered politics in Louisiana and proved to be an able leader. A delegate to the state constitutional convention, Pinchback's major achievement was the successful introduction of the Thirteenth Amendment to the state's constitution, guaranteeing civil rights to all people of the state. He was elected first to the state senate, then as its president *pro tem*. When the lieutenant governor died in 1871, Pinchback succeeded to that office. In early December 1872, Louisiana governor Henry Clay Warmoth was impeached, and Lieutenant Governor Pinchback succeeded him, serving as acting governor from December 9, 1872, to January 13, 1873. Those forty-two days made him the first African American governor of a state—and the only black to hold such a position until the election of L. Douglas Wilder as governor of Virginia in 1990.

In 1872, Pinchback was elected to the U.S. House of Representatives from Louisiana; but his Democratic opponent protested the election and won the seat. The following year, Pinchback was elected to the U.S. Senate, but charges of election irregularities thwarted his ambitions again. When Reconstruction ended in 1877, Pinchback's career in elective office ended, too. He earned a law degree from Straight University, New Orleans, and was admitted to the bar of federal and state courts in Louisiana in 1886. He moved with his family to Washington, D.C., and in 1890 organized an American Citizens' Equal Rights Association. Traveling throughout the South and Midwest, he formed local branches of the association.

Governor Pinchback died on December 21, 1921. One of his sons, Walter A. Pinchback, also had a military career. A graduate of Andover Academy and Howard University Law School, Walter Pinchback was a lieutenant in the U.S. Army and served in the infantry in the Spanish-American War.

CHARLOTTE FORTEN
GRIMKÉ

(1837–1914)

During the Reconstruction period that followed the Union victory in the Civil War, blacks in the South not only enjoyed the right to vote and hold political office, but also had the opportunity to get an education. Many schools for blacks were organized by the Freedmen's Bureau, which had been established by the federal government to assist the newly free men, women, and children.

The bureau's greatest success, wrote scholar W. E .B. Du Bois in *The Souls of Black Folk*, "lay in the planting of the free school among Negroes, and the idea of free elementary education among all classes in the South. . . . The opposition to Negro education in the South was at first bitter, and showed itself in ashes, insult, and blood; for the South believed an educated Negro to be a dangerous Negro. And the South was not wholly wrong."[1]

The former slaves joined wholeheartedly in the effort to educate themselves and their children. Many, already laboring long days to support their families, worked extra hours to build schools and pay

teachers from the first wages most newly free African Americans had ever received.

Many Northern societies, including the American Missionary Association (AMA), ~~also~~ organized black schools in the South. One of the first Northern teachers to volunteer to teach in the South for the AMA was Charlotte Forten. At the age of twenty-five she answered her nation's call for teachers.

Born in Philadelphia, Charlotte was the daughter of Robert Bridges Forten and Mary Wood Forten. She was the granddaughter of abolitionist James Forten Sr. Her father refused to allow her to attend the racially segregated schools of Philadelphia. Instead, he hired private tutors for her early education, and later sent her to the Higginson Grammar School and the Salem Normal School in Salem, Massachusetts.

Charlotte lived in the home of black abolitionist Charles Lenox Remond during her school years in Salem, and became acquainted with the anti-slavery leaders William Wells Brown, Lydia Maria Child, William Lloyd Garrison, Wendell Phillips, and John Greenleaf Whittier.

After graduating from Salem Normal School, she taught at a white grammar school in Salem, but ill health

James Forten, grandfather of Charlotte Forten Grimké, was an inventor and a successful entrepreneur, who used his wealth to help the poor and needy.

forced her to resign in 1858. She returned to Philadelphia and taught there briefly. Forten also taught one summer in Salem, but continued to be bothered by tuberculosis, then called lung fever.

In spite of her physical problems, Forten eagerly responded when the call went out for teachers in the Port Royal, South Carolina, area. She journeyed south under the sponsorship of the Philadelphia Port Royal Relief Association, one of many groups supported by Northern abolitionist societies. On October 29, 1862, she first saw the school where she was to teach. It was in a small Baptist church on St. Helena's Island, one of many islands around Port Royal. She also began a night school for the adults.

Forten became acquainted with both the officers and the enlisted men of the Fifty-fourth Massachusetts Volunteer Regiment when they were briefly stationed on the island. After their bloody attack on Fort Wagner, she traveled six miles by rowboat from St. Helena's to Beaufort to tend the wounded.

A CIVIL WAR TEACHER'S DIARY

"We went into the school, and heard the children read and spell," Forten wrote in the journal she kept for many years. "The teachers tell us that they have made great improvement in a very short time, and I noticed with pleasure how bright, how eager to learn many of them seem."[2]

Forten taught youths of all ages in the school, and gave the newly free children the first knowledge of black history they had ever received.

"Talked to the children a little while to-day about the noble Toussaint [L'Ouverture]," she wrote in her diary less than a month after her arrival. "They listened very attentively. It is well that they sh'd know what one of their color c'ld do for his race. I long to inspire them with courage and ambition (of a noble sort), and high purpose."[3]

Charlotte Forten's teaching at St. Helena's lasted until May 1864, when she returned to Philadelphia. Her health had worsened again, and she had experienced the sorrow of her father's death. Robert Bridges Forten had served in the Forty-third U.S. Colored Troops. Promoted to sergeant major and assigned to recruit volunteers, he died while on recruiting duty in Maryland and was buried with full military honors.

Charlotte Forten lived quietly for the next several years, winning minor acclaim as a writer. Two of the articles she wrote about her Port Royal experience appeared in the *Atlantic Monthly*. She returned to teaching in 1871–1872 as an assistant to the principal of the Sumner School in Washington, D.C., and then went to work as a clerk in the U.S. Treasury Department. In 1878, Forten married the Reverend Francis James Grimké, pastor of Washington's 15th Street Presbyterian Church. The couple had one child, Theodora Cornelia, who died in infancy in 1880.

Charlotte Forten Grimké spent most of the rest of her life in Washington, where she died on July 23, 1914.

CONGRESSMAN ROBERT SMALLS

(1839–1915)

The majority of blacks who fought in the Civil War served in the Union army. Robert Smalls had the distinction of serving both the Confederacy and the Union at sea. But he did not voluntarily aid the Confederate cause.

Born in Beaufort County, South Carolina, Smalls had a Jewish father and a black mother. He learned sail-making and rigging from his father. After the Civil War broke out, Smalls was pressed into the Confederate service on the ship *Planter*. As pilot, Smalls ferried supplies and munitions from Charleston Harbor out to Fort Ripley and Fort Sumter, avoiding the Union blockade.

In the spring of 1862, Robert Smalls had a daring idea. He made up his mind to hijack the *Planter*. He planned to make a run for the Union blockade even though two Confederate officers guarded the *Planter*'s black crew. Smalls and his brother John, the assistant pilot on the *Planter*, enlisted the support of the other black crew members. One night when the officers went ashore, the black crew cast off from the dock at Charleston and slowly steamed down the harbor. As the

Planter passed Fort Sumter, she fired her guns in salute. Since it was not unusual to see the ship traveling about in the early morning hours, she aroused no suspicion. The *Planter* managed to get by all the Confederate fortifications without any problem. The crew then raised a white flag signaling surrender and made their way at full steam toward the Union ships blockading the harbor entrance.

Fortunately for Smalls, the Union sailors saw the white flag just before they started to fire on *Planter*. Holding their fire, they were surprised to see only blacks aboard. Nearing the stern of the Union ship *Onward*, Robert Smalls stepped forward, took off his hat, and said, "Good morning, sir! I've brought you some of the old United States guns, sir!"[1]

The navy had accepted black enlistees even before the Civil War, but there is no evidence that either Smalls or any of his crew actually saw service in the U.S. Navy. U.S. government records show that Smalls signed a contract to be master of the *Planter* for the Union from February to July 1865. There was always at least one white Union officer on board. It was against navy policy to place blacks in command. Smalls and his crew served for the remainder of the Civil War, once narrowly escaping recapture by the Confederates.

After the war, Smalls enlisted in the South Carolina National Guard, where he achieved the rank of major general. He was a delegate to the 1868 South Carolina Constitutional Convention. He then served two terms in the state legislature and two terms in the state senate. Smalls was among the sixteen African Americans who served in the U.S. Congress during Reconstruction. Elected in 1876, 1878, 1880, and 1882, he served longer than any other black congressman of the period. Congressman Smalls died in 1915.

SERGEANT MAJOR CHRISTIAN A.
FLEETWOOD

(c. 1840–?)

Christian A. Fleetwood was born in Baltimore, Maryland, about 1840. Whether he was born free is not known, but he attended private schools. He went to Ashmund Institute, a new secondary school in Lincoln, Pennsylvania. The school later became Lincoln University, and Fleetwood was in the first graduating class in 1858.

After blacks were admitted into the Union forces, Fleetwood joined the army. On August 11, 1863, he was assigned to army headquarters in Baltimore, Maryland. Sergeant Major Fleetwood kept the soldiers' rosters and wrote reports.

Barely a month passed before Fleetwood's regiment headed out for Yorktown, Virginia. In less than a week, they were ordered on a raid. From then on, Fleetwood was in the thick of the war. There were raids once or twice a month. After April 1864, he was in Point Lookout, Maryland, guarding Confederate prisoners. Then the army formed the U.S. Colored Troops.

Fleetwood's new, black regiment was the Third Division, Eighteenth Army Troops. They built defenses, fought to hold them, and

made reconnaissances. On June 15, some 250 men in the Third Division died in battle at Petersburg, Virginia.

They again faced heavy fire from enemy guns on September 29, 1864. At Chapin's Farm in New Market Heights, Virginia, under Major General William Birney, Fleetwood and his fellow soldiers lost two-thirds of their remaining force. Fleetwood saw the two color bearers shot down. He seized the colors and carried them for the rest of the battle. For his valor, he received the Medal of Honor on April 6, 1865.

Confederate General Robert E. Lee surrendered to Union General Ulysses S. Grant at Appomattox Court House, Virginia, on April 9, 1865. Fleetwood performed garrison duty at Fort Slocum until May 1866. Then, like the vast majority of other African American soldiers, he was discharged from the army.

Soon after, Fleetwood helped found the Soldiers' and Sailors' League in Philadelphia, Pennsylvania. He settled in Washington, D.C., and taught school for a time. Then he worked with the Freedman's

WHY CONTINUE TO SERVE?

Dr. James Hall, Fleetwood's former employer, recognized his abilities and urged him to re-enlist in the army. Writing to Hall on June 8, 1865, Fleetwood explained his reluctance:

"Upon all our record there is not a single blot, and yet no member of this regiment is considered deserving of a commission or if so cannot receive one. I trust you will understand that I speak not of and for myself individually or that the lack of the pay or honor of a commission induces me to quit the service. Not so by any means, but I see no good that will result to our people by continuing to serve. On the contrary it seems to me that our continuing to act in a subordinate capacity with no hope of advancement or promotion is an absolute injury to our cause."[1]

Bank. In 1881, he went to work in the War Department. Using departmental records, he wrote about black soldiers during the Revolutionary War.

Fleetwood joined the District of Columbia National Guard, serving as captain in the Independent Company from 1880 to 1887 and as major from 1887 to 1892.

When Sergeant Major Fleetwood died, the prominent Reconstruction politicians P. B. S. Pinchback and Henry Johnson were honorary pallbearers. So was Major Charles R. Douglass, one of Frederick Douglass's sons. Fleetwood had been a member of the Frederick Douglass Post, G.A.R. (Grand Army of the Republic). After the funeral at St. Thomas Episcopal Church, he was laid to rest in Harmony Cemetery near Washington, D.C.

Proud of going to war for the Union, soldiers such as Andrew Scott paused to have their portraits made.

Senator Blanche Kelso
BRUCE

(1841–1898)

Blanche Kelso Bruce served in the Union army during the Civil War. In the Reconstruction period that followed, he was the first black person to serve a full term in the U. S. Senate.

Bruce was born to a slave woman and a white plantation owner near Farmville, Virginia. He was permitted an education and also trained as a printer's apprentice. A few years before the Civil War, his owner moved the household from Virginia to Mississippi and then to Missouri. In Missouri, the twenty-year-old Bruce escaped from slavery with two of his brothers just as the Civil War broke out.

Bruce and his brothers made their way to Hannibal, Missouri, where they tried unsuccessfully to enlist in the Union army. He then moved to Lawrence, Kansas, where he worked as a teacher and established the state's first elementary school for black children. He also attended Oberlin College in Ohio for a time and worked as a porter on a Mississippi River steamboat. In 1864, he moved to Hannibal, Missouri, and organized the state's first school for black children.

B. K. BRUCE.

A Narrow Escape

Bruce moved to Lawrence, Kansas, thinking he would be safe from recapture there. But he did not reckon on the determination of William Clarke Quantrill and his band of pro-slavery men who raided and plundered settlements of Union sympathizers in Kansas and other Midwestern states. On August 21, 1863, Quantrill's gang descended on Lawrence, burning, looting, and killing more than 150 people. Bruce was one of the lucky survivors. He moved back to Hannibal, Missouri, where he taught until the end of the war.

Not long after the Union victory in the Civil War, Congress passed the Reconstruction Act of 1867. This law placed ten southern states under military law and enabled blacks to vote and hold office. Many whites and blacks from the North traveled to the former Confederacy. Southern whites called them "carpetbaggers" (interlopers or outsiders; the nickname came from the soft satchels made of carpet material that were a common type of traveling bag at the time) and "scalawags" (rascals; the word came from the Scottish for undersized, worthless animal). Although some went for selfish purposes—to make money or gain political office—many went because they could get land cheaply, because they wanted to help the former slaves, or because they wished to claim their rightful place as citizens of Southern society.

In 1867, Bruce had gone to work as a porter on the steamship *Columbia,* traveling the Mississippi River and seeing firsthand the devastation of the former Confederacy as a result of the war. Two years later, he settled in Floreyville, Mississippi, where he was able to buy land and start a farm. Eventually, he became a successful planter. He also entered local politics and held a succession of offices, including sheriff, tax collector, and supervisor of education. By 1870 he was an emerging figure in state politics; over the next few years he served in a series of appointive offices, including sergeant at arms in the state senate. In February 1874, the Republican-controlled Mississippi legislature elected Bruce to the United States Senate.

P. B. S. Pinchback, the African American former lieutenant governor (and briefly acting governor) of Louisiana's Reconstruction government, had been elected to the Senate in 1873, but his election was still under contention. Eventually, he was denied the seat. Bruce thus was not the first African American to be elected to the Senate, but he was the first to serve a full term. (And he was the last until 1972, nearly one hundred years later, when Edward Brooke was elected to the Senate from Massachusetts.)

During his six years in the Senate, Bruce encouraged the government to be more generous in issuing western land grants to blacks who had left the South to seek freedom and opportunity in the West. He also favored distribution of duty-free clothing from England to needy blacks who had migrated to Kansas from the South. He campaigned for desegregation of U.S. Army units and for a more humane government Indian policy. He also opposed a bill to bar Chinese immigration to the United States. He urged better race relations and supported development of the Mississippi River.

By 1880, Democrats had regained control of the Mississippi legislature, and they elected a white man, James Z. George, to succeed Bruce. In the 1880 presidential campaign, Bruce served briefly as presiding officer of the Republican Party convention in Chicago, Illinois, and received eight votes as the party's vice presidential candidate.

Following the close of his Senate service on March 3, 1881, Bruce rejected an offer to be minister to Brazil because slavery was still practiced there. He accepted an appointment as registrar of the treasury and served until the Democrats regained control of the federal government in 1885. While the Democrats were in power in Washington, Bruce lectured and wrote magazine articles, and was superintendent of an exhibit on black achievement at the World's Cotton Exposition in New Orleans during 1884 and 1885. Three years later, in 1888, he received eleven votes for vice president at the Republican Party convention that nominated Benjamin Harrison. In 1889, after Harrison won election as president, he appointed Bruce recorder of deeds for the District of Columbia. Bruce served in this office for four years until 1893, then again from 1897 until his death in 1898. He was also a trustee of Howard University, which was established in 1866 as Howard Seminary to educate the children of former slaves. -

DR. CHARLES BURLEIGH
PURVIS

(1842–1929)

While Blanche Kelso Bruce persuaded Congress to assist the freedmen, Charles Burleigh Purvis worked to improve their medical care.

In the 1870s and 1880s, the death rates of black adults in the South were routinely twice as high as those of white adults, while the mortality rate of black children under the age of five was often three times as high as that of white children. In many Southern communities, one-quarter to one-third of the former slaves had died by the mid-1870s.

Charles Burleigh Purvis devoted much of his life to training black doctors to care for their people.

Purvis was one of eight children born to Harriet Forten, daughter of the abolitionist, inventor, and businessman James Forten Sr., and Robert Purvis Sr., the wealthy abolitionist and civil rights leader. Charles attended Quaker schools in Bayberry, Pennsylvania. He also learned much from the prominent anti-slavery leaders who were frequent guests in his parents' home. He attended Oberlin College in Ohio from 1860 to 1863. He then enrolled in Wooster Medical College

(later renamed Western Reserve Medical School) in Cleveland. During the summer of 1864, he worked as a military nurse at Camp Barker and saw firsthand how desperately the ex-slaves needed medical care.

Purvis graduated from Wooster Medical College in 1865. His experiences at Camp Barker may have led to his next step: enlisting in the Union army as an acting assistant surgeon. Purvis served in the Union army from 1865 to 1869, spending most of his time treating sick freedmen in Washington, D.C. He was one of only six black physicians in the city.

After serving in the Union army for four years, Purvis was appointed to the medical faculty of Howard University, becoming only the second black teacher of medicine in the United States. He was a major influence at the school for the next fifty-seven years. Known as a harsh taskmaster, he demanded that his students and colleagues keep abreast of the latest medical developments, and was impatient with anyone who did not meet his exacting standards.

On July 2, 1881, when President James A. Garfield was shot by an assassin at the Washington train station, Purvis was the first physician to treat the mortally wounded man. That action helped lead to Purvis's appointment a few months later as surgeon in chief of Freedmen's Hospital, making him the first African American to head a civilian hospital.

Purvis served at Freedmen's for almost twelve years, overseeing its growth in both size and importance. Under his leadership, the hospital became the teaching hospital for Howard University. It served thousands of patients a year, including a growing number from Southern states who were denied treatment at local hospitals because of their race.

Always the warrior for racial equality, Purvis joined with Dr. Alexander Augusta in 1869 to fight the American Medical Association's whites-only membership policy. It was a fight that African American doctors would not win until decades after Purvis had died.

Organizing Medical Care
for African Americans

Determined to do all they could to provide better treatment for their under-served people, African American doctors began to found their own hospitals, professional societies, and medical schools. From 1882 to 1900, they opened six medical schools in the South and trained approximately 1,000 doctors.

"We are all Americans, white, black, and colored," Purvis declared. "As Negroes nothing is demanded, as American citizens every enjoyment and opportunity is demanded."[1]

Purvis moved to Boston in 1905 and was admitted to the Massachusetts Medical Society. He resigned from the faculty of the Howard Medical School in 1907, but remained on its board of trustees until 1926.

Dr. Charles Burleigh Purvis died on January 30, 1929, in Los Angeles, California. He had spent sixty-five of his eighty-seven years training doctors and fighting for better medical care for African Americans.

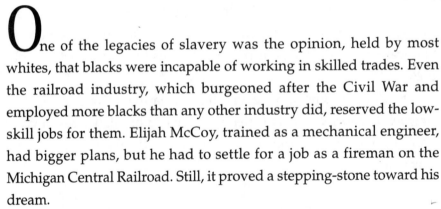

E L I J A H
McCOY

(1843–1929)

✦

One of the legacies of slavery was the opinion, held by most whites, that blacks were incapable of working in skilled trades. Even the railroad industry, which burgeoned after the Civil War and employed more blacks than any other industry did, reserved the low-skill jobs for them. Elijah McCoy, trained as a mechanical engineer, had bigger plans, but he had to settle for a job as a fireman on the Michigan Central Railroad. Still, it proved a stepping-stone toward his dream.

McCoy was born free in Colchester, Ontario, Canada, on May 2, 1843. His parents, George and Mildred McCoy, had been slaves in Kentucky and had escaped to Canada on the Underground Railroad. After a few years, McCoy's family returned to the United States, to Ypsilanti, Michigan. There, Elijah went to grammar school and worked in a machine shop.

Even as a young child, McCoy was fascinated with machinery. His parents sacrificed to send him to Edinburgh, Scotland, so that he would have a chance to learn mechanical engineering. After learning

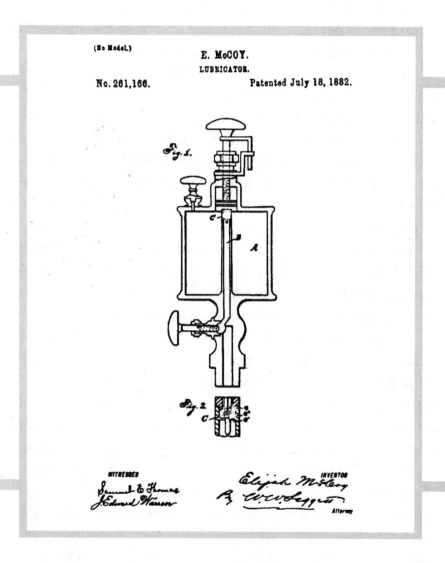

(No Model.)

E. McCOY.
LUBRICATOR.

No. 261,166.

Patented July 18, 1882.

Fig. 1.

Fig. 2.

WITNESSES
Samuel E. Thomas
J. Edward Warren

INVENTOR
Elijah McCoy
By W. W. Leggett
Attorney

everything he could as an apprentice, McCoy returned to Michigan and headed to the city of Detroit, ready and eager to find engineering work on his own.

He took the best job he could find, on the railroad. It was far from what he had hoped to do. His duties included oiling the engines of the locomotives. In those days, engines had to be periodically turned off and lubricated, or oiled, by hand. Otherwise, they would break down or catch fire. Oiling helped because it reduced the friction that made the screws, gears, levers, and other moving parts wear down.

Children, some of whom were orphans, were also hired to oil the locomotive engines by hand. Called "grease monkeys," they did dangerous work that could injure or kill them, and it often did. They were paid just pennies a day and had to sleep on the dirty, oily floors where they worked.

McCoy quickly grasped the need for a safer and more efficient method for oiling machinery. He worked daily in his crude machine shop to develop a device that would lubricate steam engines without stopping their operation and without endangering anyone.[1]

Finally, he figured out the answer. It turned out to be amazingly simple—a drip cup filled with oil attached to an engine or machine. He patented his device on July 2, 1872. Within a year, McCoy had improved the device further and had received a second patent. He assigned all or part of these patents to other people in exchange for money to pay for his workshop, and he continued to assign patents to others from then on.

At first, locomotive engineers were reluctant to use the drip cup because it was developed by an African American. But the device was so effective that they changed their minds. Within a short time, railroads, shipping lines, and factories throughout the world bought the McCoy lubricating cup. McCoy used the money he earned to develop more devices for locomotives.

THE REAL MCCOY

Around 1920, Elijah McCoy agreed to let some businessmen form the Elijah McCoy Manufacturing Company in Detroit, Michigan, to make and sell his inventions. McCoy himself worked as a patent consultant to the railroad and other industries and businesses. Other companies tried to copy McCoy products, but none met the McCoy standard for excellence. If people wanted the best quality, they learned to ask for the "real McCoy" by name.

Eventually, Elijah McCoy's inventions were recognized throughout the world. He held patents in numerous foreign countries, including Russia, France, Germany, Austria, and Great Britain. Altogether, by 1926 McCoy had received more than forty patents for his lubricating devices and other inventions, which ranged from special tires to lawn sprinklers.

Businessmen made millions selling McCoy's inventions, far more than he ever made for himself. In his later years, with fairly little money and perhaps a few regrets, he spent a lot of time working with young people, counseling and encouraging them to pursue careers in science and technology. He died in Detroit, Michigan, at age eighty-five.

THOMAS "BLIND TOM" GREENE
BETHUNE

(1849–1908)

Thomas Greene Bethune lived through the Civil War and emancipation, but he never knew freedom. Born a slave, his blindness kept him in bondage. So, in some ways, did his special musical gifts.

Today, musicians with physical disabilities, such as Ray Charles and Stevie Wonder, are acknowledged and respected. In the nineteenth century, however, a talented musician with a disability was considered an oddity. The blind pianist and composer Thomas Greene Bethune was controlled all his life by the family that owned him when he was born.

Thomas was born, sightless and enslaved, to Charity Wiggins on May 25, 1849, on the Wiley Edward Jones plantation near Columbus, Georgia. Thomas, his mother, and his siblings were soon sold to a Columbus plantation owner named James N. Bethune.

As a child, Thomas did not play much with other children—his playmate was the piano. When he was only four years old, he was discovered at the Bethune family piano, perfectly playing back songs he had heard. The technical term for this ability is "absolute pitch." Tom

had a phenomenal musical memory. He would memorize and then re-create notes and songs of all the sounds he had heard from the trees, the wind, and the birds. Some said he could even reproduce the sound of thunder.

James Bethune saw an opportunity to exploit his young slave's talents. He declared himself the manager of this "unusual" slave child and was organizing performances for Tom by the time the boy was eight. Bethune's wife was a music teacher, and she and her daughters would play piano selections by Bach, Beethoven, Chopin, Mendelssohn, and others for Thomas to play back. As he did, he steadily increased his repertoire.

In 1858, James Bethune hired Tom out to a Georgia planter named Perry Oliver, who exhibited him as "the musical prodigy of the age: A Plantation Negro Boy." His first known New York concert was on January 15, 1861, just before the outbreak of the Civil War. After the war began, Thomas was forced to give concerts for the same Confederate soldiers who were fighting to keep him and other African Americans enslaved.

Tom remained under Bethune's authority even after slavery and the war ended. Bethune had declared himself Tom's legal guardian and continued to collect whatever money the teenager earned.

THE PRODIGY

Blind Tom Bethune knew how to play nearly 7,000 musical selections. He could play all types of music, from marches, dances, operas, and ballads to plantation songs. He even composed his own music, and published some under his name and others under the pseudonyms J. C. Beckel and François Sexalise. His best-known original piece was "Battle of Manassas," named after a Civil War battle.

Tom became known as "Blind Tom" and "the human mocking-bird." Other musicians and nonbelievers in the audience constantly tested his competence. During his concerts, the audience would call out names of selections for him to play. Many came up on stage and played original work for him to repeat. Each time, Blind Tom would play back perfectly everything he had heard. He once played back a twenty-page piece while performing at the White House.

Today, Thomas Bethune would be recognized as a master musician. But in a time when most whites believed African Americans to be inferior and less than human, his superior musical abilities caused many to consider him a freak. Some historians believe he suffered from a form of mental illness. What Thomas Bethune's feelings were about his life may never be known.

Tom gave concerts throughout America under the legal guardianship of James Bethune. After James Bethune died, his son, and then the son's widow, continued to reap the financial rewards of Thomas's talents.

Blind Thomas Bethune died in 1908 in Hoboken, New Jersey. A marker placed where he was born near Columbus, Georgia, is on the list of state historic landmarks.

SERGEANT GEORGE WASHINGTON
WILLIAMS

(1849–1891)

◆

In 1860, 11-year-old George Washington Williams (born in the same year as Thomas Bethune) wrote a letter to U.S. Army General O. O. Howard. Referring to the impending war between the Northern and Southern states, he wrote that his "Hart Burned with Eager Joy to meet the Planter on the Field of Battle to prove our Human Cherater [character]."[1] By 1861 , the Civil War had begun. Three years after that, George Washington Williams, age 15, enlisted in the Union Army. He was one of the youngest men to fight in the war between the states.

Williams was born on October 16, 1849, at Bedford Springs, Pennsylvania. His father, a minister and barber, was quite well to do for a black man at the time. He traveled a lot, and his wife, Ellen Rouse Williams, worked outside the home. Young George was left pretty much on his own. It is not known if his parents were aware of their son's efforts to enlist in the Union cause. Rejected because he was too young, he determined to try again. He went to Meadville in north-western Pennsylvania, lied about his age, and registered as William Seward—or Charles Steward.

According to Williams's own account, he served for a while with the Tenth Army Corps, commanded by Major General D. B. Birney. Wounded in September 1864 in an assault on Fort Harrison, near Richmond, Virginia, Williams recovered quickly and returned to the fight. When all the black troops became the U.S. Colored Troops, Williams was assigned to the Second Division of the Twenty-fifth Army Corps. He saw action at Hatcher's Run, Five Forks, and along the sixteen-mile battle line to Petersburg, Virginia. When Petersburg fell on April 2, 1865, Williams was there. Soon after, the Confederates surrendered.

Back home in Pennsylvania, Williams probably realized that a young black man with no formal education and few skills also had few opportunities. Most of the black soldiers who had fought in the Civil War had been mustered out, and the U.S. Army had taken few steps toward making a permanent place for African Americans.

"SOLDIER OF FORTUNE"

After the war, the Twenty-fifth Army Corps went to Texas, and shortly thereafter, George Washington Williams left the army. He may have been discharged because of his age or mustered out as expected. He may have deserted. The real reason is not known.

The adventurous teenager crossed the Texas border into Mexico. Mexican general Espinosa was fighting to overthrow Emperor Maximilian, an Austrian archduke who was ruling Mexico for France. The United States was on General Espinosa's side. Williams joined Espinosa's army against the French. But it is unlikely that Williams or any of the other American soldiers of fortune who fought against Maximilian really understood the politics. Williams received a commission as lieutenant and served until the spring of 1867. Just before the final march to victory over Maximilian, Williams returned to the United States.

Regardless, Williams went to Pittsburgh and enlisted for five more years in the Twenty-seventh Infantry, under the command of Captain H. Haymond. As a drill sergeant, Williams helped get 100 recruits and then delivered them to Fort Riley, Kansas. Assigned to the Indian Territory with the Tenth Cavalry, Williams assisted in the rebuilding of Fort Arbuckle and in providing protection for settlers on the frontier. The Tenth Cavalry also campaigned against the Comanches, but it is not known whether Williams actively participated. He received a gunshot wound to his lung on May 19, 1868, but not in the line of duty. Whatever the circumstances, he was hospitalized for the rest of his time in the army.

On September 4, 1868, Williams received a Certificate of Disability for Discharge. His military career was over, and he had not yet reached his nineteenth birthday.

Following his discharge, Williams began to study for the ministry, first in St. Louis, Missouri, then at Howard University in Washington, D.C. Finally, he enrolled at Newton Theological Institution (now Seminary), in Newton, Massachusetts. In 1874, he was the first black to graduate. That same year, he also married Sarah Sterrett of Chicago and was ordained a minister at Watertown, Massachusetts. For some years, he served as pastor of Twelfth Street Baptist Church in Boston. He and Sarah had one child before their divorce in 1886.

Ever restless, Williams moved to Washington, D.C., where he started a newspaper, *The Commoner*. He then moved to Cincinnati, Ohio, where he was named minister of Union Baptist Church and wrote for local publications. He started to read law, and he was admitted to the Ohio bar in 1879. That same year, he campaigned for and won election to the State House of Representatives from Hamilton County, becoming the first black state legislator in Ohio.

While in Ohio, Williams developed a strong interest in African American history and became a voracious reader. In 1883, he published a two-volume, 1,000-page study titled *History of the Negro Race in America from 1619 to 1880.* Five years later, he published his *History of Negro Troops in the War of Rebellion, 1861–1865,* making him the first major African American historian.

In a brief eight years after his first book was published, Williams visited the Congo in Africa, wrote a landmark article against colonialism, and served as a U.S. diplomat in Haiti from 1885–1886. Later, he moved to England, where he did research. He died from a mysterious illness in 1891.

JAMES
BLAND
(1854–1911)

Unlike Thomas Bethune, James Bland was able to benefit from his own musical talents and avoid exploitation by whites. In fact, also unlike Thomas Bethune, he engaged in a bit of exploitation himself. Born free in the North, he became famous for his sentimental ballads that glorified the Old South.

Bland's parents were middle class. His father, Allan M. Bland, had been one of the first black college graduates in the United States. However, since few professions were open to a black man in America in the nineteenth century, Allan Bland was working as a tailor in Flushing, New York, when James was born.

In 1861, when James was six, the family moved to Philadelphia, where many former slaves had made their way after the end of the Civil War. They brought their music with them, and James first heard banjo music when he listened to it being played on the streets of Philadelphia by former slaves. Fascinated by the instrument and the sounds it could make, he saved up to buy one and taught himself to play.

James was fourteen when his father finally got a job that was fitting for a man of his education. It was 1868, Republicans were in power in the nation's capital of Washington, D.C., and many qualified African Americans were being appointed to federal jobs. Allan Bland was appointed to a position in the U.S. Patent Office and happily moved his family to the District of Columbia. James finished high school there and then enrolled at Howard University, which was established in 1866 to educate former slaves. He was supposed to study law, but his heart was in music.

Many former slaves worked at Howard as janitors and groundskeepers. Bland spent as much time as he could with them, listening to their stories of slavery and especially their songs. He eventually dropped out of Howard, and against his father's wishes he determined to make his living at music. He sang and played piano at parties and began composing in order to expand his repertoire. He was not yet twenty years old when he joined a traveling minstrel troupe out of Boston called the Original Black Diamonds. Over the

MINSTRELSY

Minstrelsy began around 1830 and sprang directly from the slave quarters of Southern plantations. White performers copied the styles of slave musicians, singers, and comedians—to the point of wearing blackface makeup. Their imitations were quite admiring of the rhythms and the humor of the slaves. After the Civil War and emancipation, however, white Southerners felt bitter toward the former slaves. Their imitations took on a cruel tone. By the time black entertainers were allowed onto minstrel stages, the cruel stereotypes of blacks as lazy and shiftless or as citified dudes had become so set in the public mind that blacks, too, had to act according to the stereotypes and even had to wear blackface makeup.

next few years, he worked with a variety of minstrel troupes, performing in blackface because it was expected at the time.

While with traveling minstrel troupes, Bland composed and copyrighted one of his most famous songs, "Carry Me Back to Old Virginny," at the age of twenty-four.

In 1880, Bland joined Haverly's Genuine Colored Minstrels and traveled with the troupe, renamed Haverly's European Minstrels, to Europe the following year. In London in 1881, Bland performed one of his most well-known compositions, "O Dem Golden Slippers." He found Europe a more welcoming place than his own country and remained on the continent after the Haverly troupe disbanded. For nearly a decade, he performed without blackface makeup in the leading music halls. He composed countless songs, and it was said that he could turn out a song a week.

By the early 1890s, Bland had returned to the United States. He settled in Washington, D.C., and tried to begin a new career. But musical tastes were changing, vaudeville had replaced minstrelsy as the most popular entertainment, and Bland was unsuccessful. When he died in 1911 at the age of fifty-six, he was penniless and alone.

In 1940, "Carry Me Back to Old Virginny" was chosen as the official song of the state of Virginia. Many people were surprised to learn that it had been written by a black man.

GRANVILLE T.
WOODS

(1856–1910)

"The greatest colored inventor in the history of the race, and equal, if not superior, to any inventor in the country," declared the *Catholic Tribune* in 1886. The newspaper was referring to Granville T. Woods. Inspired by the way electricity was transforming the world, Woods had unraveled the mysteries of electric currents and begun to change the world himself.

The son of Tailer and Martha Woods, Granville was born free in Columbus, Ohio, on April 23, 1856. When he was only ten, he quit school to help his family and went to work in a machine shop. Out of his hands-on education grew an enthusiasm for inventing.

At age sixteen, Woods moved to Missouri and took a job as a fireman and engineer on the railroad. An avid reader during his leisure time, he borrowed books on electricity from the local library. Friends and coworkers recognized his hunger for scientific knowledge and gave him all the books they could find on the subject. Woods practiced at work what he had learned from books.

Moving to Springfield, Illinois, and then to New York City, Woods found work wherever he could, first in a steel mill and then in another machine shop. But his heart was set on going to an electrical and mechanical engineering school where he could take real courses, and eventually he did.

With his new knowledge, he secured a job as an engineer on *Ironsides*, a British steamship. He worked on this ship for two years, until a job as an engineer on the Danville and Southern Railroad took him away.

By 1881, Woods was ready for a new challenge and opened an electrical equipment factory in Cincinnati, Ohio. After years of working in positions that were beneath his abilities, he believed that he could fare better as his own boss. He worked diligently for two years. On June 3, 1884, at the age of twenty-eight, Woods received his first patent. It was for an improved steam-boiler furnace for steam-driven engines. On December 2, 1884, he received another patent, this time for a stronger, clearer telephone transmitter. It set a new direction for his imagination.

In 1885, Woods patented a device that combined the telegraph with the telephone. Woods called it a "telegraphony." Instead of reading or writing the Morse code signals, an operator could speak near the telegraph key. This device made it possible to receive both oral and signal messages clearly over the same line without making changes in the instrument and without understanding Morse code. Woods's telegraphony was purchased by the American Bell Telephone Company of Boston, Massachusetts, for a large sum of money.

Woods continued to explore the power of telegraphy. His next invention, patented on November 15, 1887, allowed conductors and engineers on moving trains to send and receive messages for the first time.

With this success, the inventor formed the Woods Electric Company. Orders for his devices came in from around the world. In 1890, Woods moved to New York City and joined his brother, Lyates

SEEING THE PROBLEM

New Yorkers, including the Woods brothers, loved to go to shows. But theaters had become fire hazards. Why? The electrical system that slowly dimmed the lights and controlled the other electrical equipment could easily become overheated.

Woods decided to focus on the problem. Through careful study and experimentation, he discovered a way to dim the lights using a separate generator. By controlling the strength of the electrical current, this system eliminated the overheating problem. Woods patented his theater lighting system on October 13, 1896.

Woods, also an inventor. They made a brilliant team. By 1907, Granville Woods would have some sixty patents to his credit.

A few of Woods's inventions stood out from the rest. Some people considered the "third rail" to be his greatest invention. Used in subway systems throughout the world, the third rail put electrical conductors along the path of the train so that the cars would receive the current directly without needing an electric engine. On January 29, 1901, Woods received a patent for the "third rail," and he sold this invention to the General Electric Company of New York shortly after.

Other people believed that Woods's air brake technology was just as important as the third rail. Starting in 1902, he had developed several devices that led to the automatic air brake. Woods eventually sold this system to the Westinghouse Air Brake Company of Pennsylvania.

Called the "Black Edison," Woods faced as many difficulties as victories and never rested on his laurels. Once, in 1892, he was arrested and kept in jail in connection with charges he himself had brought against the American Engineering Company for stealing one of his patents. Legal fees he could barely afford and powerful enemies in business and politics made his life a struggle right to the end.

He died of a stroke in 1910 and was buried in New York City.

BOOKER T. WASHINGTON

(1856–1915)

During Reconstruction, blacks gained freedom, the right to be educated, and the right to vote. But soon, through violence, fraud, and legal tricks, black people in the South lost virtually all the rights they had gained. Public schools that had been opened to them were closed. Without the right to vote, there was little they could do about it. Booker T. Washington, an educator, struggled to find a way to help his people make progress in the hostile post-Reconstruction South.

Booker Taliaferro Washington was born into slavery on April 5, 1856, in Franklin County, Virginia. His mother, Jane, was enslaved, and his father was a white man he never knew.

When he was nine years old, he was sent to work in a salt mine by his stepfather, a man named Washington Ferguson, whom his mother married sometime after Booker was born. Between the ages of ten and twelve, Booker also worked in coal mines near his home in Malden, Virginia, as did many other children at the time. The work was hard and dangerous.

Eager to learn, Booker managed to obtain a little schooling before and after work. His mother also arranged for the teacher from the local black school to give him lessons at night. As he recalled years later, "[we were] a whole race trying to go to school. Few were too young, and none too old, to make the attempt to learn. As fast as any kind of teachers could be secured, not only were day-schools filled, but night-schools as well."[1]

One day while working in the coal mine, he heard two miners talking about "a great school for coloured people somewhere in Virginia. . . . As they went on describing the school, it seemed to me that it must be the greatest place on earth."[2] The school was the Hampton Normal and Agricultural Institute (later Hampton Institute). In 1872, the eager 16-year-old began the 500-mile journey to the school, walking most of the way.

His decision to enroll in Hampton was probably the most important one of his life. The school's principal was General Samuel Chapman Armstrong, a man who had commanded black Union army soldiers in the Civil War. He quickly befriended Washington and arranged for a white northern philanthropist to pay the young man's tuition. Washington earned his room and board by working as a janitor at the school.

Washington said he received two great benefits from his years as a student at Hampton: the friendship of Armstrong and the knowledge of the importance of vocational education, the teaching of skilled trades.

Washington graduated from Hampton in 1875 and returned home to Malden to teach. In 1879, he went back to Hampton to teach in a program for Native Americans, where he remained for two years.

In 1881, through the influence of General Armstrong, Washington was offered a position that would bring him worldwide fame: the principalship of a high school to train black teachers in Tuskegee, Alabama. The school had been authorized by the Alabama legislature, and the twenty-five-year-old Washington quickly accepted the offer. But when he arrived, he found that the legislature's $2,000 appropriation covered only salaries. There were no school buildings or land.

He recruited students from throughout the county, and held the institute's first classes in a shanty near a black Methodist church. The church was used as an assembly hall. Washington said the shanty was in such poor shape that "whenever it rained, one of the older students would very kindly leave his lessons to hold an umbrella over me."[3]

All of Tuskegee's buildings were constructed by the students. Washington determined that they "would be taught to see not only utility in labour, but beauty and dignity."[4] By 1888, Tuskegee owned 540 acres of land, had an enrollment of over 400, and offered courses in printing, cabinetmaking, carpentry, farming, cooking, sewing, and other vocational skills. Washington believed that practical, vocational education gave people skills to make a living as well as independence and self-reliance.

Washington was not the first black educator to teach the virtues of self-reliance, though none did it more successfully. His name

THE PRINCIPAL BUILDS HIS SCHOOL

A personal loan from the treasurer at Hampton Institute enabled Booker T. Washington to buy an abandoned plantation on the edge of Tuskegee, Alabama. The mansion on the plantation had been burned down, but the Tuskegee students repaired a stable and a henhouse for use as classrooms. Black residents in the area contributed whatever money they could toward buying materials for a new building. One farmer who had no money gave a "fine hog."

A white sawmill owner supplied the lumber, even though Washington could not pay him until much later. With this help, and money from several whites in the North, Washington put the thirty students to work erecting Tuskegee's first new building.

Tuskegee students gather for a history class in one of the many classrooms built with the skillful hands of students.

became a household word throughout the country, however, for another reason. In his "Atlanta Compromise" speech on September 18, 1895, at the opening of the Cotton States and International Exposition in Atlanta, Georgia, Washington urged black Americans to accept segregation and its second-class status.

He declared: "The wisest among my race understand that the agitation of questions of social equality is the extremest folly."[5]

Black members of the audience wept openly at this surrender of their dreams of equality, but the majority of white Americans loved the speech. White editorial writers and politicians took it upon themselves to proclaim Washington the new black leader (Frederick Douglass, the leading African American for decades, had died a few months before).

John D. Rockefeller, Andrew Carnegie, and other wealthy industrialists contributed money to Washington for black education.

The legendary educator Booker T. Washington poses with a group of Tuskegee Institute teachers and trustees.

Presidents Theodore Roosevelt and William Howard Taft consulted him on which black Americans should receive governmental jobs. But Washington's critics charged that his opposition to nonvocational academic training for black people would keep black people on the bottom rungs of society's ladder.

Though Washington publicly told black people to accept segregation, he fought behind the scenes to end it. His work encouraging an investigation into black peonage (semi-slavery) in Alabama helped bring about a federal court ruling that it was unconstitutional.

In 1904, Washington secretly financed a legal challenge against Alabama for denying qualified black people the right to vote. He supported successful appeals in an Alabama case involving the exclusion of black people from a jury. He also helped challenge transportation laws requiring separate seating for blacks and whites. These actions were accomplished so carefully that few black people, and almost no white people, knew about them.

In the latter years of his life, Washington was helped at the institute by its principal—his third wife, Margaret Murray Washington. They were married in 1893. Washington's first wife, Fannie M. Smith, had died in 1884 after two years of marriage. They had one daughter. In

1885, Washington had married a second time, to Olivia A. Davidson, the assistant principal of Tuskegee. She died in 1889, leaving him two sons.

Washington passed away at Tuskegee from heart disease on November 14, 1915, at the age of fifty-nine. His funeral, held three days later in the Tuskegee Institute Chapel, was attended by almost 8,000 people.

CHRONOLOGY

1619   First Africans arrive in British North American colonies, sold as laborers in Jamestown, Virginia

1700   Enslaved population in British North America is 27,817, of which 22,600 are in the Southern colonies

1759   Enslaved population in British North America is 230,000, still mostly in the South

1775   First abolition society formed in Philadelphia

1776   The Revolutionary War begins

        The Declaration of Independence

1783   The Revolutionary War ends

1797   Sojourner (Isabella Hurley) Truth born

1806   Sarah Mapps Douglass born

1812   Major Martin Robison Delany born

1815   Lieutenant Peter Vogelsang born

1818   Elizabeth Keckley born

        Frederick Douglass born

1820   Harriet Tubman born

1825   Frances E. W. Harper born

        Dr. Alexander T. Augusta born

1827   John P. Parker born

1833   Phildelphia Female Anti-Slavery Society founded

1837   Governor Pinckney Benton Stewart Pinchback born

        Charlotte Forten Grimké born

        Francis Louis Cardozo born

1839   Congressman Robert Smalls born

c. 1840   Sergeant Major Christian A. Fleetwood born

1841   Senator Blanche Kelso Bruce born

1842   Dr. Charles Burleigh Purvis born

1843   Elijah McCoy born

1848   Susie King Taylor born

1849   Sergeant George Washington Williams born

        Thomas "Blind Tom" Greene Bethune born

1850	Of the nearly 400,000 free blacks in the United States, 3,000 own land
1853	Harriet Beecher Stowe's *Uncle Tom's Cabin,* a book on slavery, sells over 300,000 copies in the United States in its first year of publication
1854	James Bland born
1856	Granville T. Woods born
	Booker T. Washington born
1857	In the case of *Scott* v. *Sandford,* the U.S. Supreme Court rules against citizenship for blacks
1860	Abraham Lincoln of Illinois elected President of the United States
1861	Seven Southern states secede from the Union and form the Confederate States of America; the Civil War begins
1862	Robert Smalls hijacks the Confederate *Planter* and delivers her to the Union navy
1863	President Abraham Lincoln issues the Emancipation Proclamation, which frees the slaves in the secessionist Confederate States of America
	Fifty-fourth Massachusetts Volunteer Regiment mustered into service
	Fifty-fourth Massachusetts Volunteer Regiment assaults Fort Wagner, South Carolina
1865	Martin R. Delany is the first black man to receive a regular army commission
	The Civil War ends; President Lincoln is assassinated
	Reconstruction begins
1866	Congress authorizes the first peacetime units of African American soldiers; the Ninth and Tenth Cavalries are nicknamed "Buffalo Soldiers"
1871	Pinckney Benton Stewart Pinchback succeeds to the post of lieutenant governor of Reconstruction Louisiana
1872–1873	For forty-two days, P. B. S. Pinchback serves as acting governor of Louisiana
1875	Federal Civil Rights Act gives blacks the right to equal treatment in public places and transport
1876	Robert Smalls elected to Congress; reelected in 1878, 1880, and 1882, he serves longer than any other black congressman of the period
1877	Reconstruction ends
1882	Sarah Mapps Douglass dies
1883	Sojourner Truth dies
	U.S. Supreme Court declares 1875 Civil Rights Act unconstitutional

1885	Major Martin Robison Delany dies
1887	Lieutenant Peter Vogelsang dies
	Southern states begin to pass segregation laws known as "Black Codes"
1890	Dr. Alexander T. Augusta dies
	Southern states begin systematic exclusion of blacks from politics
1891	Sergeant George Washington Williams dies
1892	Between 1892 and 1901, more than 100 black Americans are lynched, or illegally executed, by whites each year
1895	Frederick Douglass dies
1896	U.S. Supreme Court rules in *Plessy* v. *Ferguson* that separate but equal accommodations for blacks and whites are constitutional
1898	Senator Blanche Kelso Bruce dies
1900	John P. Parker dies
	Federal census records African American population of the United States as 8,833,994
1903	Francis Louis Cardozo dies
1907	Elizabeth Keckley dies
1908	Thomas "Blind Tom" Greene Bethune dies
1910	Granville T. Woods dies
1911	Frances E. W. Harper dies
	James Bland dies
1912	Susie King Taylor dies
1913	Harriet Tubman dies
1914	Charlotte Forten Grimké dies
1915	Booker T. Washington dies
	Congressman Robert Smalls dies
1921	Governor Pinckney Benton Stewart Pinchback dies
1929	Dr. Charles Burleigh Purvis dies
	Elijah McCoy dies

NOTES

MAJOR MARTIN ROBISON DELANY

1. Waldo E. Martin, Jr. *The Mind of Frederick Douglass* (Chapel Hill: University of North Carolina Press, 1984), 95.

LIEUTENANT PETER VOGELSANG

1. Peter Burchard. *"We'll Stand by the Union": Robert Gould Shaw and the Black 54th Massachusetts Regiment* (New York: Facts on File, 1993), 85.

FREDERICK DOUGLASS

1. William S. McFeeley. *Frederick Douglass* (New York: W.W. Norton & Co., 1991), 213.
2. Bruce Levine et al., eds. *Who Built America? Working People and the Nation's Economy, Politics, Culture, and Society,* Vol. I (New York: Pantheon Books, 1989), 513.

HARRIET TUBMAN

1. Patricia E. Romero, ed. *Reminiscences of My Life in Camp* (New York: M. Wiener, 1988).

DR. ALEXANDER T. AUGUSTA

1. Ira Berlin, ed. *Freedom: A Documentary History of Emancipation, 1861–1867* (New York: Cambridge University Press, 1982), 354.
2. Ibid., 355.

FRANCIS LOUIS CARDOZO

1. "The South as It Is," *The Nation* (1865), 779.

GOVERNOR PINCKNEY BENTON STEWART PINCHBACK

1. James M. McPherson. *The Negro's Civil War* (New York: Ballantine, 1991), 159.

CHARLOTTE FORTEN GRIMKÉ

1. William E. B. Du Bois. *The Souls of Black Folks,* in William E. B. Du Bois, James Weldon Johnson, and Booker T. Washington, *Three Negro Classics* (New York: Avon Books, 1965), 234.
2. "A Social Experiment: The Port Royal Journal of Charlotte L. Forten, 1862–1863," *Journal of Negro History* (July 1950), 242.
3. Gerda Lerner, ed. *Black Women in White America: A Documentary History* (New York: Vintage Books, 1973), 96.

CONGRESSMAN ROBERT SMALLS

1. James M. McPherson. *The Negro's Civil War* (New York: Ballantine, 1991), 189.

DR. CHARLES BURLEIGH PURVIS

1. Rayford W. Logan, ed. *Dictionary of American Negro Biography* (New York: W.W. Norton & Co., 1982), 508.

ELIJAH MCCOY

1. United States Patent Office, Application for Automatic Lubricator Patent, July 2, 1872.

SERGEANT GEORGE WASHINGTON WILLIAMS

1. John Hope Franklin. *George Washington Williams, A Biography* (Chicago: University of Chicago Press, 1985), 3.

BOOKER T. WASHINGTON

1. Booker T. Washington. *Up from Slavery,* in William E. B. Du Bois, James Weldon Johnson, and Booker T. Washington, *Three Negro Classics* (New York: Avon Books, 1965), 44–45.
2. Ibid., 51.
3. Ibid., 68.
4. Ibid., 87.
5. Ibid., 108.

PICTURE CREDITS

Author Credits

Key:

Entrepreneurs: Jim Haskins, *African American Entrepreneurs* (New York: John Wiley & Sons, Inc., 1998).

Military Heroes: Jim Haskins, *African American Military Heroes* (New York: John Wiley & Sons, Inc. 1998)

Musicians: Eleanora Tate, *African American Musicians* (New York: John Wiley & Sons, Inc., 2000).

Teachers: Clinton Cox, *African American Teachers* (New York: John Wiley & Sons, Inc., 2000).

Writers: Brenda Wilkinson, *African American Women Writers* (New York: John Wiley & Sons, Inc., 2000).

Inventors: Otha Richard Sullivan, *African American Inventors* (New York: John Wiley & Sons, Inc., 1998).

By Jim Haskins

Major Martin Robison Delany, Lieutenant Peter Vogelsang, Harriet Tubman, Governor Pinckney Benton Stewart Pinchback, Congressman Robert Smalls, Sergeant Major Christian A. Fleetwood, Sergeant George Washington Williams adapted from *Military Heroes;* Elizabeth Keckley, adapted from *Entrepreneurs;* Frederick Douglass, John P. Parker; Senator Blanche Kelso Bruce.

By Clinton Cox

Sarah Mapps Douglass, Charlotte Forten Grimké, Francis Louis Cardozo, Booker T. Washington adapted from *Teachers;* Dr. Alexander T. Augusta, Dr. Charles Burleigh Purvis, adapted from *Healers.*

By Eleanora Tate

Thomas "Blind Tom" Green Bethune, adapted from *Musicians.*

By Otha Richard Sullivan

Elijah McCoy, Granville T. Woods, adapted from *Inventors.*

By Brenda Wilkinson

Soujourner Truth, Frances E. W. Harper, adapted from *Writers.*

INDEX